Bagzof money

content

Live By It
Die By It

II

Ice Money

Live By It, Die By It II

Printed in the United States of America.

ISBN: 978-1-7366158-3-6

Table of Contents

Acknowledgments

I would like to give praise and thanks to Allah, the most gracious, most merciful for giving me the ability to articulate these words in the way I do. I pray that he continues to guide and bless me through my successes as well as my failures.

I would like to extend my appreciation to those who have supported and encouraged me to keep these novels flowing: shout out to B.O.M Content and the record label, So Geeked Records, of which I serve as Vice President and shout out to my city, Milwaukee, Wisconsin—MKE, stand up! I would also like to send my deepest condolences to those who have been victims of police brutality and injustices all over the world, such as Derrick Williams, Joel Acevedo, George Floyd, Breonna Taylor, Ahmaud Arbery, Eric Garner, Mike Brown, Botham Jean, Antwon Rose Jr., Tamir Rice, Rayshard Brooks, Trayvon Martin, and Julius Jones, just to name a few, as well as their families. These outrageous deaths and injustices truly showed how divided our country still is... and how oppressed the black race is. Slavery has been abolished for over four hundred years, yet there are racist flags hanging damn near in every state. There are slavery monuments glorified all over the country, as if telling us "niggas, don't forget where you came from".

I was beyond elated when I seen those things being pulled down, broken, defaced, and dumped into the lakes and rivers. It showed me black people have arisen; we are sick and tired of being sick and tired. We are ready to let the world know it. I smiled when I seen the people in Iraq with signs that said BLACK LIVES MATTER, and we do, the world is hearing us! United WE stand, divided WE fall... It's a shame we have to tell them that BLACK LIVES MATTER because our lives have ALWAYS mattered! They just continued to hold us back, we told them we couldn't breathe, but they kept their knees on our necks or kept us in a chokehold. We just wanted to go to the store for a drink, but we never made it home to drink that drink. We riding in the car with our women and kids, but you made sure we didn't get to see our kids graduate. It's just ridiculous, and so counterproductive, coming from the people for whom we provide a salary with our tax dollars. It seems like all over the world, black people have always endured the absolute worst. Even the coronavirus outbreak is affecting black people more than any other ethnicity.

I yearn for the day when we are truly treated equally, as the brother, Dr. Martin Luther King Jr. preached so resolutely about. Even blacks who have matriculated, have endured harsh things, yet, they have gone on to establish beautiful educations and careers for themselves in the face of racism... all due to the color of their skin. They are listening, so our voices must continue to be heard. I want to personally thank all the people over the world who have protested injustices, racial biases, the over population of black people in the corrupt prison systems. For CHANGE, which was Barack Obama's campaign slogan when he became the first black

President, that was something to remember, but if you think he was beyond being subjected to racism because he was the POTUS, you're very naive. The crook in the White House now continues to promote racism. He can't even hide it if he wanted to. He like a pot of something boiling, it's bound to spill over... still shaking my head about him being in that spot in the first place, when I just knew he'd be out by the primaries, but like I said, that just shows how divided our country still is... Continue to push, I see great things for us as a people, Al-Humdu Allah (praise God).

#BLM   #NoJusticeNoPeace   #SayTheirNames

Shout out my A-1's who I am in constant contact with... AP3, Louise Telus, Fookie, Quinn, Terrell, Dennis, Blanco, LJ, JB, Rocko, Eshawn, Cordé, Mac, Cuervo, Wakil, PeeWee, Javi, and Ace Boogie.

Chapter One

* * * * *

"Did you hear me?" he shot at her.

"Yeah, I heard you, you said you trust me, right?" she turned to face him, and when she opened her eyes, she was staring down the barrel of his .45 caliber pistol. He pulled the trigger and the right side of her face exploded, splashing blood on the dashboard and onto the bullet-shattered window before her body slumped back into the seat. Richie Rich had to take her out because she knew too much. She became more and more reckless by the minute, and he couldn't afford to have any loose ends. If he was gonna play the game, he had to play it. He had to follow the code, if he was gon' live by it, he was prepared to die by it.

Richie Rich leaned over her, opened the passenger's side door, and pushed her lifeless body out, letting it slap against the pavement before he closed the door. He then started the car, and without hesitation, smashed off. Richie Rich made a left out of the parking lot and sped down Green Bay Avenue until he reached Capital Drive and made a right. As he drove, he couldn't help but think about his lack of judgement and awareness that ultimately got his loved ones taken away from him. Now, nothing could replace their lives, but he'd be lying if he said he didn't feel a strong vindication after knocking everybody off that was responsible for his grief and eliminating any possibilities for the streets to start talking. Now, it was time for him to reintroduce himself back into the game, and thanks to the fifty grand in the duffel bag that he got out of Chauncey's trunk, things would be much simpler.

When he heard something beeping, he looked at the gas gauge, and realized the tank was damn near empty. Distracted by his thoughts, he snapped back into reality and realized he was trippin' hard with no map, riding around with a hot ass pistol, in a stoley with blood all through it. *I gotta get rid of this car*, he thought to himself just as he passed 24th & Capital. He almost shat on himself when he heard the howling of a siren. His eyes quickly shot to the rearview mirror to see an ambulance pulling into traffic from a side street. Richie Rich let out a sigh of relief as he turned down 26th Street, drove down to Hope Street, rounded the corner, then came up the alley, and parked behind the gas station on 27th & Capital. After peeping the scenery, he tucked the gun away, hopped out the car after wiping his prints, and went to the trunk. Looking inside, he grabbed a t-shirt, shut the trunk, and went to stuff it under the driver's seat. Reaching in his pocket, he retrieved the lighter, set the shirt on fire, and nonchalantly walked off after making sure the flame got bigger.

Richie Rich darted across the street towards McDonald's to use the pay phone, so he could call a taxicab. When he made it to the entrance, he reached for the door and looked back. He saw a fine, dark-skinned female heading towards him, so he held the door open, and followed that with "How you doin' today?"

As she passed him, she smiled with a polite gesture, and responded with "I'm good" while she kept walking. Richie Rich took her in. She was stunning, she heavily favored the beautiful Sub 0° Phat Puffs model Hersey Lust with the voluptuous and bodacious body to match. Richie Rich was about to leave it at that, because he was just trying to use the phone and get up outta there, but she looked too damn good to pass up. Besides, he knew the best things came when you weren't looking for them, so he walked over to her while she stood in line after ordering her food. "Excuse me, can I share a few words with you?" he asked. Turning around, she said "Sure... I guess" with a funny expression on her face. "I apologize for coming off so aggressive, but when I see a woman so sexy and appealing, I feel like I need to know her" he offered and looked directly into her eyes.

"Why?" she responded in a snobby tone. She gave him the once over. Richie Rich knew she wasn't the typical woman by her response and by how she carried herself. He had been around women long enough to pinpoint the THOTs from the real women, because real women have a halo of confidence, poise, and tranquility, which she had. Never the one to give up in pursuit of what he wanted, he stayed persistent. "Because I think you're worth the challenge, so let's introduce ourselves to one another over a meal" he said. She gave him a puzzled look, but he was quick on his feet. "You can pick the place; therefore, you'll feel safe enough to relax" he pressed on.

"First off, I'm not worried about you doing anything to me, secondly, if I do say yes to getting something to eat, why is it that you want me relaxed?" she inquired. Richie Rich ignored her hard-to-get attitude. "It's a date, then" he smoothly replied. "I'ont even know yo name" she added. "Richie Rich" he said, introducing himself.

"Boy, please" she rolled her eyes, having none of it.

"What's yo name while you ridiculing mine?" he pointed out, but continuing the exchange.

"Danita, but everybody calls me Nita" she answered. Richie Rich nodded his head. "I'm feeling that" he replied, while laughing "You thought I was gon' say something slick, didn't you?"

"Naw, 'cause my Mama knew what she was doing" she laughed. After talking for a few more minutes, she started feeling his presence and sense of humor, and decided to give him a shot and see what he was on.

"So, are you gonna give me your number or do you want mine? I gotta get goin" she said while picking up her phone off the counter. "Imma need yours because I gotta get another phone" he answered.

She glanced at him again, "Richie Rich, huh? But you don't have a cellphone, and I saw you walking across the street when I pulled up, so that means you don't have a car either" she said, her sarcasm evident. "It's a long story, but, believe me when I say I'm good" he replied, loving her jazzy attitude. "I've heard it all before, only because of yo cute face Imma give you my number, and we'll soon find out how good you really are" she said while scribbling her number on a napkin, handing it to him, then she turned to leave after grabbing her food.

Richie Rich just stared at her five-foot five-inch frame, she had smooth chocolate skin, big breasts, wide hips, and thick thighs with a sassy walk to go with all that ass she had as she headed to a burgundy Chrysler 300C. When she got in, she lowered the window while putting the car in reverse. "Don't call me super late at night talking about dinner either because this ain't that, so don't try it" she said, letting him know that if he was just calling her late to go eat in hopes that she would be his desert, he had another thing coming.

"What you talkin' ab—" he started to say with his hands up, but she cut him off. "You heard me" she said then smashed off, turned up Capital, and disappeared into traffic.

Richie Rich stood there stunned and impressed all at the same time as thoughts of Jamillah entered his mind due to the strong resemblance of characteristics that she and Nita shared as she vanished in traffic. When Richie heard the sound of a fire truck, he looked towards the gas station and seen the thick heavy dark smoke coming from behind the station, and he knew that was his cue to get up outta there as he ran across the street and walked down 27th Street towards Locust.

Chapter Two

*****

Three days later...

Hello, he answered.

"Quincy..." he added.

Who dis? he asked, wanting to be certain.

"Richie Rich" he replied.

Aw, what's good boy, I ain't heard from you in a minute, that's kinda odd for a nigga of yo status, everything good? Quincy said.

"Hell yeah, I been outta commission for a minute, but now I'm tryna get back on my feet, you know how it go" Richie replied.

I feel that, Quincy paused. *Well, throw some numbers at me*, he added getting right down to business because he knew whenever Richie Rich called, it was about money.

"I need to holla at you face to face today, if you ain't too busy" Richie continued.

That's cool, when you wanna meet up? Quincy asked.

"Meet me at PT's in forty-five minutes" Richie said, getting ready.

You still love that place, huh? Quincy said, letting out a chuckle.

"It's just a comfort thang, that's all" Richie replied.

Aight, I'll see you then, Quincy said, ending the call.

Richie Rich went into the backroom and got dressed in a pair of indigo blue jean Balenciaga shorts with the belt, white, orange, and blue Balenciaga T-shirt, and threw on the Balenciaga shoes to match his attire. Now, Richie liked these shoes a lot, they were stylish, he just hated how they always messed his socks up. Reaching inside his nightstand drawer, he pulled out an ounce of OG kush, rolled up a blunt, and immediately set flame to it. Going in the living room, he sat on the couch and ran his hand over his waves as he continued to puff the blunt before picking up the bottle of Patron Silver that was on the table and gulped down two large swallows.

Today was RJ's birthday and, since he couldn't be there to celebrate for himself, Richie Rich was going to do it for him. A couple of days ago, he went to get RJ and Jamillah's faces tattooed on his back next to his parents with R.I.P and the respective dates of their arrival and departure from earth. Richie Rich said a prayer for them and followed that up with two more gulps of his bottle, quickly feeling the effects as it burned the back of his throat all the way down getting him to where he needed to be, he smiled. Once he started to feel like a million bucks, he grabbed his new iPhone 8 and dialed one of the four numbers stored inside.

Hello, her sweet voice sounded like music to her ears.

"Danita there?" he asked already knowing it was her on the other end.

This is she; may I ask who is calling? she added.

"Richie Rich" he replied.

Oh heyyy, I thought you forgot about me, she said after a brief pause.

"Neva that, what you on today?" he asked her.

Nothing, why? she asked while switching him to speaker phone.

"I'm finna head out and catch up on some business, and I was wondering can I slide yo way once I'm done to take you out to that dinner I promised" Richie Rich said. He then took a puff of his blunt as he heard giggling in the background. "Never mind, I see you got company" he said.

It's not company like that, boy, it's just my friends from Chicago, Ciera and Tiera, she added.

"Ciera and Tiera" he replied in a mocking tone.

Yeah, they twins, why you say it like that? he asked.

"Listen, Nita... to be honest, I don't really give two fucks about that. It's just that after I take care of this business, I'ont know what time it's gon' be and I'ont want you waiting on me all day, so should I call you later on?" he asked.

I'll probably have to see you tomorrow then, plus I'm with my girls, and I told you don't be tryna call me late at night, she reminded him.

Richie Rich looked at the phone with his face screwed up before he spoke. "I'll catch up wit you some other time then because clearly it's a misunderstanding" he said.

Do that th— she started to say but he ended the call.

"This nigga hung up in my face" she said in disbelief as Ciera and Tiera laughed. Danita couldn't believe him, but she wasn't tripping as she tossed her cellphone on her living room table.

I ain't got time for her games... Richie Rich thought to himself as he took several more pulls of his blunt before placing it in the ashtray. Getting up, he threw the phone on his bed, went in his closet, grabbed the book bag, and started counting out money. He had a little over ninety-six thousand to his name, and that was the money he grabbed out of his safe, what he took from Chauncey, and after he sold his Benz truck, but that's why he was going to meet Quincy, so he could get his line back slappin', the trap back jumping, and get his money up.

Stuffing six thousand in his pocket, he put the rest of the money back in the book bag, put his 'Garfield' chain on his neck, his iced out white gold Hubolt watch on his wrist, his big boy buff Cartier tinted glasses with diamonds in them on his face, put his diamond earrings on, and put his white, orange, and blue Balenciaga cap on his head. Putting his phone in his pocket, he stuffed the .40 extendo in his waistband. Grabbing his keys and bookbag, he left out the door.

He smiled when he saw the sun dancing off of RJ's all orange '85 Cutlass Supreme with the blue quarter top. Richie Rich had put the 28-inch Forgiato rims on it, the pair he took off the Lesabre that he bought from Jamillah's cousin Lil Mickey and gave to Chauncey. He was gon' do a little jackin' in his brother's honor today. Hitting the alarm, he opened the trunk, threw the book bag next to the two 15-inch L-7 Kicker Subwoofers, closed it, and hopped in the car. Starting it, he lowered the tinted window, pulled off from his new house with the sound of the duels growling as he turned from 42nd & Greentree heading to PT's. Getting a decent distance from his house, he put in Milwaukee artist Party Boi's mixtape 'I Love Haters' and put it on the track 'Glazin' featuring Kia Shine and B.E. Pulling up to the lights on Mill Road & Teutonia, Richie Rich swerved the wheel from side to side as the Patron started to kick in. The sunlight reflected perfectly off of the custom paint and big rims, drawing attention from everyone.

"Happy Birthday, bro, rest in peace" he said to himself as he pulled off bobbing his head. Pulling up to the intersection on Teutonia & Villard, he made a right, and eased up off the exhaust as his heart almost jumped out of his chest when he saw the police sitting in the back of McDonald's about to exit. He used his remote to hit mute on the radio and put both hands on the wheel. Although he wasn't driving reckless, he was a young black man in a ghetto fabulous car on eights, a few Gs in his pocket, another ninety thousand in the trunk with no job. He was behind tints, had a burner on him, and he was little tipsy, all of that was a recipe for a disaster. Even though he had Ls, the weed had him a little paranoid. When he passed them, he immediately looked in his rearview mirror, and let out a sigh of relief when he saw the cops remain sitting there. Making a left on 35th Street, he drove down, and pulled up in PT's parking lot. Looking around he spotted Quincy's black Yukon parked in the spot closest to the building. Richie Rich pulled next to the truck, jumped out, hit the alarm, and went into the club.

Chapter Three

* * * * *

When Richie Rich walked into the club, it was semi-packed. 'Thick' by O.T. Genesis and 2 Chainz thumped out of the speakers. Every table he passed occupied two or more people, there was people everywhere, and money was definitely on display. Females were in there showing off their red bottom shoes and dressed in the latest Chanel, Dolce & Gabbana, Cavalli, Fendi, and other high-end apparels. Then you had those who were in there with discount store dresses on acting like they were top notch, knowing they weren't. Everybody knows that in Milwaukee, niggas who really checkin' in a bag, always go out dressed like they were attending a fashion show or walking in one. So those who were in there wore things from low-end apparel to the exclusive stuff that was only being sold in New York. Nevertheless, you couldn't tell a nigga nothing who thought he was fresh to death. Tables were covered in Ace of Spades, Dom Perignon, white Remy, and then you had the traditional bottles of Patron, Rosé Moët, Ciroc, Wasted Vodka, and Hennessy, so variety was definitely not a problem, if you drank it, PT's had it.

Richie Rich proceeded through the club, until he heard somebody call his name, looking in the direction where it came from, he smiled, and headed in their direction.

"What's good, Party Boi?" Richie Rich said shaking his hand. Party Boi was a light skinned nigga who was off the trays too and getting to the bag. Truth be told, he was the next to blow outta Milwaukee on the music side.

"Shit, it's good to see you back out here" Party Boi said.

"I appreciate that, fam, you know how it is when you knee deep in the mud and wit some niggas who ain't wit you, but while they fucked up. I'm still out here buffed up, you feel me?" Richie smirked as he adjusted his glasses.

"Hell yeah, I already know how it is" Party Boi nodded.

"I got the new mixtape in the car, that shit goin' hard too" Richie added.

"Nice lookin', you know I'm out here grindin'. Aye, this my brother Amazin, my brother Segal, my cousin Big Bank, my cousin D, and my cousin JR, you know it's a family affair wit me, I can't wait for my brother Ice to touch, and shit really gon' go down" Party Boi introduced everybody. Richie Rich shook their hands, he had seen a couple of them in the hood, but didn't know them, but all these niggas looked and smelled like money.

"I saw yo videos on 414 Video Spotlight last week too, you did yo thang too" Richie complimented. "Melvin James a good dude, he be showing love to the city, so I try to support that however I can" Boi added.

"Fo sho, Imma get up with you, though, my dude" Richie Rich said before shaking everybody's hand and leaving. Richie Rich spotted P.T. at the bar throwing back shots with several young ladies. Richie Rich smirked then made his way towards the back where he saw Mac and some of his guys, they were off & Capital. They were at a table with plenty of bitches, bottles, and bands. Richie knew most of them and they'd sell some dope, but he knew that Mac had them bitches in there to take advantage of any opportunity, whatever it was. When Mac looked up from the chick in his lap, Richie Rich acknowledged him with a head nod, and Mac replied by patting his chest with the 'H' letting him know it was all love, then he got right back to his business.

After saying what up to a few other cats that he knew in the club, he finally spotted Quincy sitting off near the corner, but he wasn't sitting alone, there was two other dudes sitting with him that Richie had never seen before. Quincy spotted Richie Rich coming in his direction and stood up causing the two dudes he was with to turn and look.

"Long time, no see" he said shaking Richie Rich's hand.

"Likewise, but money is still the motive" Richie replied.

"You knew that, but what you wanted to holla at me about?" Quincy inquired.

Disregarding his question, Richie nodded his head towards the two guys that were sitting at the table. "Who dat?" he asked.

"This uhh, Greg" Quincy said pointing to one of the dudes. "And that's JC" he pointed to the other dude. "These my dudes off 24th & Vienna, they good peoples and strictly about cash" Quincy said. He paused for a second as he looked around the club. "Let's get down to business, bro" he continued.

Richie Rich had been buying work from Quincy for a minute now, and he was always a straight up dude as far as he knew, so he didn't question his decision to bring his guys along. As they took their seats, Richie Rich hesitated for a second to gather himself because anything he ever wanted, he bought because money wasn't a problem for him, but now he wasn't in a position to do that due to the robbery, so he laid his proposition out on the table in hopes that Quincy would give him the benefit of doubt. "After that lil bullshit, my finances wouldn't allow me that luxury, plus my expenses for the shit I gotta have, I..." he was saying until Quincy cut him off.

"You ain't gotta go through all that, just tell me what I can do for you" Quincy offered.

"Okay, I got ninety for you right now if you can slide me three, but I need you to front me three more on consignment and I'll hit you on the re-up" Richie said.

Quincy sat back in his seat running his hand over his goatee while doing some mental math in his head. "You know what? I know how it is out here when you on the rise and niggas start hatin' and shit. You always came correct on the money side and I know you be gettin' that shit off, so I got you, but under one condition, and if you say yes, Imma sweeten up the pot" Quincy reasoned.

Richie Rich dropped his head and chuckled before he looked up, smiled, and said "What is it?" Quincy leaned in and placed his hand on Richie Rich's shoulder, displayed a bold smile. "Imma give you my last 10 slabs on consignment for two hundred and fifty thousand on the back end, but JC and Greg trappin' wit you until I get back from outta town" he said.

"What!" Richie Rich said feeling ecstatic about the deal, but skeptical and uneasy about what, -rather who- was attached to it. "Fam, I'ont even know these dudes to be puttin' 'em in my bidness like that" he added while leaning back in his chair looking at Quincy, never acknowledging JC or Greg. Quincy looked over to JC and Greg, then back to Richie Rich. "Put it like this, these my dudes and theyre just watching my investment. I gotta head down to Texas, then swing around to Arkansas, and hit Atlanta, and it's gon' be like two or three weeks. It ain't like they gon' be standing over yo shoulder, they just there til I get my two fifty. Take it or leave it" he shrugged his shoulders.

Richie Rich took a second to respond as he weighed his options, but he fully understood that if he was gonna rebuild his clientele the right way and lock Milwaukee down, he was gonna need that work to return to CEO status. On top of getting the ten birds, he'd get to keep his ninety k, he'd be a fool not to take that offer, he had too. Richie looked over at Quincy, resolute. "Fuck it, we got a deal, Imma have yo boys overseeing this neighborhood Imma put them in with no questions asked right?" making sure they fully understood the deal. It sounded fair to Quincy as long as he got his money in the end, but just for the hell of it, he looked to his guys. "Y'all got a problem with that?"

"I'm here to get money, anything else is irrelevant" JC replied.

"I'm here for you, so if that's how it's gonna be...then so be it" Greg followed up.

"We good then, fam, I'mma hit yo line tomorrow to set up the drop spot" Quincy said. "But in the meantime, get us some drinks over here" he added.

"Let's get this money, fellas" Richie Rich said leaning over and shaking JC and Greg's hand, then he signaled for a waitress. "About what time you wanna meet up in the morning?" he asked Quincy.

"Around ten o'clock" Quincy replied.

"That's perfect" Richie Rich said just as the waitress walked up. "What's yo name?" he added while looking her up and down.

"Chocolate" she answered.

"You must be new here?" he replied while thinking that she looked like the sexy Porsha Williams from the Real Housewives of Atlanta in the face.

"Yeah, I just started yesterday" she said taking in everybody at the table.

"Well, Chocolate, it's nice to meet you, sexy, they call me Richie Rich" he said going into his pocket, pulling out the six Gs, and peeling her off three of them. "Bring me a bottle of Ace of Spades, Ciroc, Hennessey, and a Moët Rosé. Tell that group of strippers to get over here and get this money and tell the DJ to throw on something they can twerk to, and keep that change, aight" he told Chocolate.

"I got you, Richie Rich" she smiled before walking off throwing that thang. Richie Rich watched her as she walked off to do what he asked and she had an ass like a horse, his manly instinct told him one day that he'd have to see what that do.

Quincy was leaning back in his seat trying to see why Richie Rich loved this place so much instead of the clubs downtown where niggas his age hung out at, and he figured it had to be because of the variety of women walking around butt ass naked. JC felt it was time to see what Richie Rich had in mind, but when he tried to get his attention, Richie gave him the cold shoulder, and Greg peeped it, so he stepped up. "Say man, how you wanna do this?" he asked, irritation dripping from his words. Richie Rich caught how he asked him the question but stayed composed. Richie thought for a minute, he had to find a way to keep these dudes outta his mix since he just had to kill his best friend for doing some shiesty shit. He certainly wasn't ready to partner up with some niggas that he didn't even know, so he'd put them in a place where they'd be outta his face, in place to make money, and close enough to where he could watch them, so after taking that into consideration, he figured it out.

"Imma put y'all in control of the South Side" Richie said.

"The South Side!" JC and Greg said in unison.

"Yeah, it's plenty of money to get over there, that is what we're doing this for, right?" he replied and before he could say another word 'Anaconda' by Nicki Minaj came bumping through the speakers. When Richie Rich turned, Chocolate was walking up with the bottles he asked for, four glasses, and four strippers in tow. "We'll talk more about this tomorrow, right now, it's party time" Richie said, looking towards JC.

"Pass me that Henny, I'm drinkin' out the bottle, fuck that glass" Quincy said as Chocolate put the bottles on the table. After downing the bottles and several lap dances later, Quincy decided to call it a night. Tapping JC and Greg on the shoulder, he let them know it was time to bounce. Before they left, Richie Rich stored JC's number in his phone and told him that he would get up with him tomorrow. Richie Rich sat back observing the scene, thinking to himself just how he was going to go about reestablishing himself back into the game, and have longevity. First things first, he knew that he had to keep his circle extra tight.

Reaching in his pocket, he, peeled off a few hundred and waved to get Chocolate's attention. When she walked up, he passed her the money. "Aye, take a bottle of some of that good shit to my nigga Party Boi over there." he pointed, but she already knew who he was. "Tell him I said to drink up, I'm back out here" he said.

"Is that right?" she replied.

"You damn right, I'm known to put numbers up on the scoreboard, so you may need to give me yo number, Imma give you my jersey, and put you on this winning team" he flirted with her.

"It ain't that easy, but hopefully I'll see you around and we can kick it sometime" she said batting her eyelashes.

"No doubt, baby girl, I like yo style and if I catch you in traffic, we surely can kick it" Richie continued.

"Well, you know where I work" Chocolate said, throwing him a devious smile.

"Point made" he said then walked off with his sauce on extra drip because he knew she was watching him.

As he was walking, he felt a pair of eyes on him, he looked to see Fatty Mack, Jamillah's cousin at a table with plenty of niggas, hoes, and money mugging him. Since Richie Rich had gotten out of the hospital, he heard that Jamillah's family blamed him for her death, and truthfully, he did feel responsible, but he wasn't tryna get into it with Fatty, that was his nigga, he learned a lot about how to play the game and win from Fatty, but when the time was right, he was gonna get up with him and holla at him, but this definitely wasn't the time or place to do it.

Passing Mac's table, he watched two females count their earnings and slide it to him discreetly under the table. Mac looked up, nodded at Richie Rich who nodded back as he headed to the exit. *That nigga got them hoes cashin out, I must be in the wrong profession, but ain't no money like trap money...* Richie Rich thought to himself.

Chapter Four

The night was still young for Richie Rich; he felt like Milwaukee wasn't sleeping, so why should he? Feeling like a new man with a master plan, he was speeding down Sherman Boulevard intimidating traffic with the duals hollering as he weaved in and out of traffic. He pulled Lil Baby's latest CD '2 The Hard Way' from the deck and popped in Moneybagg Yo's 'Federal 3x' CD in and turned on the song 'Reckless' featuring Young boy Never Broke Again and cranked the volume and as it blasted out of his subwoofers, he rapped the chorus along with Moneybagg Yo word for word.

I just popped a bean

I just threw my neck back

I'm in the latest machine

I hope I'ont wreck that

Bitch threaten me like she gon' leave

Cool ain't gon' sweat that

You ain't never got no time for me

I hate when she text that

I just got flagged by the law

I just had a minor setback

Honey honey with my dogs ten to four

I'm like bet that

Aye I'm at the paper

I'm at that, neck and wrist is on wet wet

Hit the clear port where the jects at/name one thing I ain't best at...

Getting caught at the lights on Sherman & Fond du Lac, he sat behind the steering wheel swerving it from side to side jackin' hard behind tint while sitting on the big 28-inch stilts. When a pair of headlights came into his rearview, he pulled himself together and put his pistol on his lap just as the car pulled up on his left side preparing to turn left and go down Fond du Lac Avenue. Richie Rich watched the burgundy car as it came to a stop, he noticed it was occupied by three females. He blew his horn, but they were already looking at the attractive car with the five-thousand wet paint job and big wheels with the music so loud that it sounded like it had a marching band in it. He smiled while watching them wave and gesture for him to lower his window so they could see him.

Suddenly, the light turned green in the process, but neither car pulled off. Richie Rich lowered his window just enough to stick his hand out and point in the direction they were going so they knew to pull over. The girl in the passenger seat got geeked up shaking her head up and down. Seeing this, Richie Rich knew off top she wanted to fuck his car.

The driver pulled off turning left, but she didn't pull over right away. instead, they went up to the lights and pulled into the gas station on Townsend Street. A few seconds later, Richie Rich pulled up glazin', duals growling with his music shaking the gas station windows. Dipping around, he pulled up on the other side of the pump they were at in the opposite direction. Turning his music down, he hopped out saucey as fuck and straightened the Balenciaga hat on his head, before stuffing the ratchet in his waistband, which was required although he was having fun, he knew Milwaukee was a grimy city and he'd rather be judged by twelve than be carried by six any day. Coming around the gas pump, he was so throwing back when he seen the driver that he just shook his head and smiled in disbelief. The driver opened the door and stood up with a fulfilled smirk when she seen him. Richie Rich knew she was impressed once she got a glimpse of the real him in his element.

"Well, well, well, if it ain't conceited, smart mouthed ass Danita." he smiled.

"No, you didn't" she replied with a dumb ass look on her face as her friend in the passenger seat got out.

"Girl, you know him?" she asked Nita.

"Something like that, Tiera" she replied.

"You lucky, cause I had something for his ass" she eyed him on her way back to the car. Richie Rich could tell that she was the freak out of the clique because every group of girls at least had one or two of them. Richie Rich disregarded her comment because chicks like her came a dime a dozen, and he was used to having money. Focusing his attention back on Nita.

"So, what up wit you?" he asked.

"What do you mean, you the one that hung up on me" she said rolling her neck making him laugh.

"Naw, you seemed to be distracted with yo friends. All I was tryna do was take you out, I didn't think that I deserved all that attitude I was getting" he said. Feeling like she had been too hard on him, she tried to clean it up.

"Well, you didn't say that when you..." she started but he cut her off knowing what she was about to say.

"Because you ain't let me finish, you gotta give yo ears the same chance you give your mouth and since you didn't do that, we ended up turning something positive into something negative, you feel me?" he reasoned.

"So, how can we fix it then?" she asked.

"I know you don't get a second chance at first impressions, but I was hoping that we can start over, let me introduce you into my world, and if you wit that, we can go from there, if not, we can say our goodbyes right here with no hard feelings" he said with his hands out.

Nita paused for a second, although she had a slick ass mouth, she wasn't no damn fool. Here she was being pursued by a man that seemed to have his shit together and genuinely liked her for her as far as she could tell, she couldn't let her attitude get in the way of this, so she softened up thinking that if he was serious, she was going to give him a shot.

"Well, sometimes second chances are better than the first, so when can we go get that dinner?" she asked.

Richie Rich shook his head hoping that she would see things his way. "We definitely gon' do that, Imma hit yo line, now be safe out here and get home" he said.

"Where you going?" Nita replied.

"I got business to take care of" he said.

"I thought you handled that already?" she said checking the time on her cellphone.

"A true businessman is really never off work, matter of fact, you got Ls?" he asked, and she nodded. "If you ain't busy tomorrow, let me pay you to drive me somewhere" he added. Nita already knew what time it was when he asked her if she have a driver's license, but she played it cool.

"That's cool, I could use the money" she was about to say something else, but she followed Richie Rich's eyes as he observed more cars pulling into the gas station causing his survival instincts to kick in. They probably wasn't on nothing, but at 2:00 am, niggas be having that liquor courage and he wasn't the one to be playing with, so just to avoid an altercation altogether which could get ugly, he decided to get up outta there.

"Gon head and get in yo car, Imma hit you in the morning around nine o'clock" he said walking around the pump, hopping in his car, and putting his pistol on his lap. Once Nita pulled off, he skidded out of the parking lot while turning up 'What Your City Like' by Tee Grizzley featuring Lil Durk.

******

Pulling up on 24th & Vienna in front of JC's crib, Quincy asked JC and Greg about their opinion of Richie Rich. Greg said that he heard of Richie Rich, but he wasn't impressed by what he saw thus far. JC said Richie Rich seemed cool to him and he didn't think he'd have a problem working with him. Quincy told them both not to interfere with Richie Rich's offense, just let him maneuver things the way he liked to so there wouldn't be any bullshit in the game while he was outta town. They agreed to play the wing to Richie Rich for Quincy and hopped out of his truck.

"I'll holla at y'all in a couple of weeks and hit my line if you need me before then" Quincy said.

"Aight, you be easy down there, luv" JC said shutting the door. Greg threw the deuces up as Quincy smashed off hitting his horn.

On their way into the house, JC patted Greg on the back. "Be cool fam, we just gon' do us, as long as the money comin' in, we all good" he told Greg.

"I'll be good, I just don't like that nigga Richie Rich square ass, he too damn cocky. Imma play the background but he bet not eva get slick wit me and if he do, on my nigga, Imma fuck him clean up" Greg replied. JC just shook his head and walked into the house.

Chapter Five

* * * * *

The sun pierced through the curtains as the morning dew started to evaporate and streams of water ran down the window. Richie Rich opened his eyes, stretched while yawning, then he reached over and grabbed the half blunt out the ashtray and a liter to have the appropriate hood nigga wake up. Lighting the blunt, he inhaled deeply and held it as he laid back staring at the ceiling contemplating on just how he was about to put his plan into motion. After deciding he couldn't do nothing while lying on the bed, he got up, and headed to the shower to get himself together. About ten minutes later, he went to his closet to find something to wear. Deciding on a pair of black Maison Margiela sweatpants, a royal blue Maison Margiela T-shirt, and his #11 'Space Jam' edition retro Air Jordans, he got dressed. After strapping his white gold and diamond Rolex wristwatch on, he decided to call Nita to see if she was up getting ready because he knew how long females took to get ready.

Hello, her voice cracked through the phone signaling she was still asleep.

"Don't nothing come to a sleeper but a dream, so let's get up and get it together" he said.

What time is it? she asked after his voice registered and she knew who it was.

"Ten minutes to nine, so chop chop" he laughed.

Boy, don't rush me, beauty takes time, she replied, smiling.

"You're a natural, it don't take that long" he said making her blush.

Quite the charmer, aren't you? I'm getting up now, she added.

"Gimme yo address so I can come scoop you" he replied.

I don't usually let dudes know where I stay at, she explained to him.

How Imma come get you then if I don't know where you live? Stop playin' and tell me where you live at" he said while rolling up another blunt.

I'm in the high rises on 27th…

"27th & Fond du Lac. That's why you don't want nobody to know where you live at, you live in the damn ghetto" he laughed.

Well… she said feeling a little embarrassed.

Sensing her being embarrassed, he cleaned it up not wanting to offend her. "I'm just fuckin' wit you, what floor you on?"

I'm on the third floor, but you don't have to worry about ringing the buzzer because I can see you from my window when you pull up, she said.

"Ay, you right by the Chaney Center, them niggas be out there posted up working out actin' like they on somethin' tryna catch, don't they?" he joked.

Yeah, they do, but at shit moving, at least not with me, she added.

"You smoke? "he asked firing up his blunt.

Smoke what? she asked.

"Don't run that innocent shit on me, I know you just as ghetto as that street you live on" he laughed while stuffing five Gs in his pocket.

Whatever, she smiled.

"I'll be there in like forty-five minutes. I gotta go holla at my lil brother, and then I'm on my way" he told her.

Don't keep me waiting, she said.

"I won't, I promise" he said ending the call.

Stuffing a quarter ounce of moon rock kush in his pocket, he tucked his F&N extendo in his waistband, grabbed his keys, and left the house. Getting in his Trail Blazer, he started it, put on his big boy Cartier glasses with the diamonds and tinted lenses, turned up the volume on his factory speakers to

'Key To The Street' by YFN Lucci featuring Migos and Trouble, and pulled off bobbing his head.

Pulling up on 32nd & Silver Spring, he made a right, pulled almost to the end of the block, and hit the horn as he parked. About a minute later, Jacoby came rushing out of the house and hopped in the truck wit Richie Rich. "What's good, bro?" Coby said smiling.

"Chillin', every time I see yo azz it seems like you getting bigger and bigger, how tall is you now?" he said.

"6'4" and I'm 200 pounds. I think I can fold you up now" he said throwing a playful jab.

"Don't let that height and weight get yo azz whooped, I'm still the big brother" Richie Rich said as they laughed "You been looking into them colleges? Yo senior year of high school gon' fly by next year, so you gotta be ready" Richie Rich said removing his glasses.

"Yeah, I'm thinking about going to Kentucky. John Calipari been recruiting me hard, he came to one of my games last season, I was so geeked, I just went off for 41 points" Coby said.

"Oh yeah, how many assists did you have?" Richie asked.

"Like four" he replied.

"Four?" he asked.

"I had seven boards too, but I scored forty-one points, so I didn't need to pass that much" Coby said making Richie laugh. "They started calling me show by after that game because they said I be showing out" he added.

"You a fool wit it, lil bro" Richie said.

"I got letters from Coach K outta Duke, Bill Self in Kansas, Roy Williams in North Carolina, and Coach Wojo in Marquette, but I'm not sure I wanna go there, Auntie wants me to leave the state. That's why I said Kentucky because it ain't that far and my guy AP3 who I play AAU with talking about going there, he cold too, and our games mesh together, so we should turn up together, but I'm not a hundred percent right now" Coby said shaking his head.

Richie Rich looked at his little brother and could see him maturing before his eyes, he was glad that he didn't fall victim to the street life like he did. Coby had a God-given talent with the basketball and Richie Rich was glad he was focused on that. "Where you rank in the state?" Richie Rich asked.

"The preseason polls got me ranked number two behind this 6'9" dude named Michael Foster Jr. who goes to Washington High School, he a savage and I think he's going to Arizona State, he had a great freshman year even though he got skipped, from seventh to ninth grade, but Imma turn up and mid-way through the season, I should be number one, but AP3 on my heels to, he rank number 3, he good azz point guard, and a lefty too" he said knowing he was gonna have to bring it to get that number one spot. "I had a job at Foot Locker, but I gotta leave for LeBron's camp in Vegas next month, so I ain't gon' be able to take it. Speaking of LeBron, you see that hoe azz shit Kyrie pulled asking for a trade?

Talking about he don't wanna play with Bron no more, that shit crazy" Coby said.

"Yeah it was, he gon' see how hard it is to be the best man on a contending team, that shit is not easy, I'ont know where they gon' trade him, but on Sports center they said Boston has the most assets to trade for Kyrie, so we'll see, I know Bron pissed, came back got this nigga name buzzing, I mean we all know kyrie got that shit, but he never been in the playoffs until Bron came back, he got Kyrie shoes being the number two selling shoes in the league, and he tryna leave, that's gon' bite him in the azz tryna outshine the master" Richie Rich said.

"I hope Bron get some more help, he a free agent after next season anyway, so if they don't get it together, you already know he don't have a problem leaving. I'm tryna see him get five or six rings, putting him in a position to be better than Jordan, but right now I got Jordan number one and Bron number two all time."

"I feel that, that's how I got it too." Richie smiled. "Auntie working today?" he added.

"Yep, she won't be home until like 5:00 pm" Coby said.

        "Aye, where that sexy yellow girl at with the glasses and all the tattoos who stayed across the street wit the two little brothers?" Richie Rich asked.

"They been moved" Coby answered.

"Oh, I always wanted to hit that, but did you do that for me?" Richie asked.

"Yeah, pull around the back by the garage" Coby said as Richie Rich started the truck and pulled into the alley next to his Aunt's garage. Jacoby hopped out of the truck, went into the garage, and raised the big door up. Then he backed Richie Rich's royal blue 2013 Dodge Challenger SRT8 with the navy-blue soft convertible top out of the garage. Richie Rich smiled when he seen his baby as he got out of his truck. He bought the car, fixed it up, and got his Auntie to let him store it in her garage until the summertime. He had been intending to bring it out, but between getting shot and trying to get back on his feet, he hadn't had time until now. Richie Rich walked over to the car and rubbed his hands on the Pirelli tires that held the chrome 28-inch Forgiato rims in place and smiled because he knew the car was a one of one as he opened the door and put his pistol, glasses, and CD on the seat.

"I cleaned 'em up good, bro" Coby said hopping out.

"Hell yeah, good lookin'" Richie Rich said as his phone rung, looking at the screen he saw it was Quincy, so he quickly answered. "What it do?" he said mildly trying not to sound anxious.

I know we said ten o'clock, but somethin' came up and I gotta ride out earlier than expected, so can you meet me now? Quincy asked.

"I'm finna go pick my driver up now and then Imma slide right on you, where you want me to meet you at?" Richie asked.

Meet me at Foot Locker's parking lot on 3rd Street, I'm in my Lac truck, if you ain't there in forty-five minutes, I'm gone, he replied.

"Aight, I'm on my way" Richie Rich said ending the call. "Bro, how that Grand Prix holdin' up?" he added as he texted Nita, letting her know that he was on his way.

"It's okay" Coby said.

"Well, you can have this truck, it's clean, I only had it for a couple months. I got two pair of Jordans in the Finish Line bag in the back with an envelope that has two thousand dollars in it. If you need anything else, bro, all you gotta do is hit my line and Imma be there ASAP" Richie promised.

Coby couldn't hide his excitement as he went over and hugged his brother tightly. "I love you, bro" he said.

"I love you too, lil nigga, now get off me wit that emotional shit, I gotta get outta here. Keep them grades up and keep working on your game, you never too good not to practice hard" Richie Rich said.

"Aight" Coby said and shook his hand before Richie hopped behind the wheel of his Challenger.

"The key's in the ignition, title in the glove box, just hit me up later on" he said while putting his Cartiers back on.

"Imma do that" Coby said as Richie Rich pulled off. Getting on 35th Street, Richie slid his mixed disc in the Pioneer deck. 'Super Trapper' by Future thumped out of the three 15-inch

JL Audio subwoofers in his trunk as he moved swiftly through traffic bobbing his head on his way to Nita's house.

Chapter Six

* * * * *

When Richie Rich pulled up, he was surprised to see Nita standing out front waiting on him. When he saw her, he couldn't help but to picture Jamillah due to their resemblance. In the couple encounters that Richie Rich had with Nita, he really liked her style, personality, and how she carried herself. Richie Rich felt like she could potentially be the one for him, so he was going to take the necessary steps to see if she had the criteria to be with a man like him. Richie Rich took off his glasses as he watched Nita strut towards the car putting an extra umph in her hips that were clearly protruding through her jeans. He couldn't understand how she was so thick, and her waistline was so little. When Nita opened the door and slid in, Richie Rich took in her sexy hazel brown eyes highlighted by her thick perfectly arched eyebrows and her pretty smile that complimented her natural beauty.

"You look nice, sweetheart." he said looking her over. She wore a pair of curve-flattering jeans by Michael Kors, a white 'MK' halter top that exposed her mid-section and navel ring, a pair of white open toe Michael Kors sandals adorned her pedicured feet, and her hair was on point with box goddess braids.

"Thank you, and so do you" she smiled. "I was about to go back in the house because I didn't know this was what you were driving, I thought it was somebody tryna holla, and I ain't in the mood for that. How many cars do you have?" she added.

"Just a few, I just had to show you how straight I really am since you doubted me when we met at McDonald's" they shared a laugh. "You ready?" he continued.

"Yeah, where we going?" she asked feeling entitled to know as Richie Rich threw the car in park and hopped out. "What are you doing?" she added.

"You driving, remember?" he told her.

"You letting me drive this?" she smiled as he grabbed her white Michael Kors handbag, got out, and walked around the back of the car. As she passed him, he looked at her voluminous ass and shook his head while thinking, *Damn... she thick as fuck.*

"I hope you know what you doing behind the wheel on these eights" he said over the top of the car.

"I haven't drove on no big rims before, but it shouldn't be that hard" she reassured him.

"Aight, don't tear my shit up" he smiled.

"Boy, gone" she said collapsing on the navy-blue Ostrich seats, then adjusting it to fit her comfortably.

"We gon' ride in style" he said hitting the button to let the top back.

"I never seen a drop top Challenger before" she added.

"Fuckin' wit me, you gon' see a lot of things you never saw before" he licked his lips then smiled making her blush.

"Ride down to Foot Locker on 3rd Street" he continued then put his Cartier back on and adjusted his seat.

When he looked back towards Nita, she was rambling in her purse until she pulled out her big Chloe shades and some lip gloss. Flipping the visor down expecting to use the mirror only it was a TV right there, flipping it back up, she looked at the outside side mirror but that was a TV too, so she used the rearview mirror and shook her head when she seen a quarter of that mirror was a TV as well, not to mention the one that was in the steering wheel. "You got too many TVs in here." she said putting her lip gloss back in her purse and rubbing her lips together.

"It's only eight, now let's ride out" he said as she dropped the gearshift into drive, hit the peddle, then immediately hit the brake, and looked at Richie Rich because she wasn't expecting the car to have that much torque.

"Yeah, that's a V8 with a Hemi, that shit serious" he smiled. Determined to show him that she could handle it, she pressed lightly on the pedal, but it didn't make a difference. As she turned on Fond du Lac, it was like the car had a mind of its own storming through the early morning traffic. Richie Rich pulled out a blunt of kush, told her to roll up the windows then he changed the aroma in the air and leaned back in his seat.

Looking over to Nita, he damn near wanted to laugh when he seen her sitting straight up, seat belt on with her hands at 10 and 2 on the wheel with pure concentration on her face. "Here" he passed her the blunt. "Relax a little, baby" he continued. Never taking her eyes off the road, Nita reached over, grabbed the blunt, took a few small puffs, and handed it back to him.

"That's more like it" he said grabbing the blunt, then he turned his sub's up. 'Jam' by Kevin Gates featuring Trey Songz, Ty Dolla $ign, and Jamie Foxx came on bumping hard sounding like Gorillas were in the trunk trying to get out, Richie Rich cut it down a little and leaned back watching everything as Nita drove East down Wright Street. Making a right on 4th Street, the drove down to North Avenue, made a left, then hit a right, before hitting another left and pulling up in Foot Locker's parking lot. Richie Rich immediately spotted the Lac truck parked all the way in the back blending in with the other vehicles.

"Back in right here" he told her, so they were still in view of the truck. "Keep the car running, I'll be right back" he added while gently squeezing her thigh then hopping out of the whip.

Nita watched Richie Rich as he walked over to a Cadillac truck, she loved the strong presence, command, and confidence he exuded. Although they had not known each other for that long, she trusted her womanly intuition when it told her that he could be the one for her, he displayed all of the signs so far. She smiled hoping that he was in the same thought process as she watched him jump in the back of the truck.

"What up, my dude?" Quincy said handing Richie Rich a book bag, then pointing to the one that was behind the passenger's seat. "Grab that one too" he added.

Reaching down, Richie Rich grabbed the bag and noticed a pistol with an extended clip sitting on the passenger's lap, but he didn't say a word, nor did he look back. Positioning both bags on his lap, Richie Rich grabbed the paper that Quincy was holding out for him.

"That's JC and Greg's numbers, they ready to move when you say so" Quincy said.

"Aight, I'll catch up wit you as soon as you get back." Richie Rich said opening the door and getting out.

"No doubt, I see you pulled out the drop Challenger, that muthafucka hard too, what you want for that?" Quincy asked smiling.

"It ain't for sell yet, I just pulled it out, I gotta break it in first" he smiled.

"Let me know, I want that" Quincy said.

"Aight" Richie Rich smiled as he closed the door and Quincy backed out and pulled off.

Richie Rich walked back to his car carrying both bags like groceries. Nita saw what he was carrying, and her heart started to race as she looked around because she knew that he either had plenty of weed or dope.

"Pop the trunk" he said while passing the car. Placing both bags in the trunk, he got back in the passenger's seat, and shut the door. Normally a person would get a low-key car for carrying that much work, but he felt like those were the cars that got sweated the most, so he did the opposite of what everybody else did.

Richie Rich looked over to Nita who didn't say a word, she just sat there waiting on directions. When he asked her to let him put the bags in her house since it was closer, she felt like this was his way of trying to build something with her through the trust factor. "That's fine if you need to" she said.

"Do you have anything you need to do today?"

"No" she answered.

"After we drop these bags off, I'mma need you to drive me to the cellphone shop so I can get another line" Richie said knowing that he had to display some form of trust in her if she ever had what it took to be with a street nigga like himself.

"Alright" she said. Richie Rich eyed her closely and sensed the loyalty in her demeanor, she carried it like a boss chick, and he loved that. After peeling back a few layers, he understood that she put up her walls of protection to keep the essence of her womanhood safe, probably due to someone not recognizing her value and worth, so they mistreated her causing her to put up those walls of defense. Richie Rich didn't want her to think like he was even remotely close to any dude she had in her past, so he knew he had to present himself in a different light, which he had no problem doing. He wanted her to feel safe and comfortable around him, so he went with his instincts and somewhat made it official with her.

"Listen, Nita, I know it's only been like a half day we spent together straight... Obviously you're a very attractive woman, but I feel there's something here worth exploring deeper than the physical. Now, I don't even know if this is an option for you, but I wouldn't be keepin' it real with myself if I didn't tell you that I like what I've seen thus far and I wanna take it a step further and see if we can build on that if you give me the opportunity to" Richie Rich spoke.

Nita just sat there staring at him trying to come up with the right words to complement what he just said. She knew he was serious about what he said, because the tone he said it in, and the stern look on his face. However, she wasn't able to come up with the right words. She knew actions spoke louder than words, so she placed her hand on his leg, leaned forward, grabbed the back of his head, and gave him a passionate kiss on the lips.

"Imma hold you down and be the woman you need me to be, I just ask that you don't fuck me over, because I—" she was abruptly cut off.

"I understand, you gon' be in good hands, I promise you that, now let's get outta here" he said before reaching under her seat and grabbing his pistol, then he hit the button to raise the roof back up.

Nita put the car in drive and pulled off while Richie Rich looked out of the window. "Here I come, Milwaukee" he said to himself.

Chapter Seven

* * * * *

Richie Rich's Rollie read ten minutes to eleven after dropping the merch off at Nita's house, then he had her take him to the cellphone shop so that he could get another line. After grabbing a couple of soul food plates from Perkins' Family Restaurant on Atkinson Avenue, they returned to Nita's apartment. As they pulled up in front of her building, Richie Rich could tell the traffic outside was picking up, and he also noticed the unmarked police car sitting off the corner watching several dudes that were posted up on 26th Street. The scene wasn't ideal for Richie Rich, but he already had his dope inside of the apartment, so he had to go in. Richie Rich tucked his .30 so it couldn't be seen before he stepped out of the car. When Nita got out the car, she hit the alarm, then the "Aye, shorty", "Damn" and whistling began.

Richie Rich just smirked because she was just that bad. While walking to the building, one of the grimy looking dudes out there was mugging the hell outta Richie tryna size him up, but that wasn't nothing new to him, because everywhere he went, he had a nice car, bad chick, and looked like money, so niggas see that and try to do little shit to intimidate you, so they could get a read on you to see if you were wit the shits or not. So, every time that happened, Richie would respond the same way, by staring back with a stern look on his face, displaying no signs of being intimidated or weakness whatsoever, until whoever it was that was looking turned their head which dude did, but before he did, Richie caught him looking at his hip, he must've also seen the .30 round stick Richie was trying to conceal under his shirt poking out. Shaking his head, he opened the door to the building for Nita, and then followed her inside.

Once they made it upstairs into her apartment, Richie Rich looked around and admired her taste in furniture, from the sectional couch, the curtains, lamps, end tables, rugs, and the 20-gallon fish tank with an assortment of tropical fish that looked like they were straight outta the movie 'Finding Nemo'. "You have a nice place here" he complimented. "What do you do for a living?" he added.

"Thank you, I'm a social worker, I work with at-risk youth from 12 to 25" she said before going into the back room.

"Sexy and sophisticated" Richie Rich said as he grabbed one of the book bags, sat it on the kitchen table, and unzipped it to see what he was working with just as Nita entered the kitchen tryna be nosy and see what was in the bag.

"You not expecting anybody, is you?" he asked trying to make sure nobody was going to pop up while he had all that dope in her house.

"If anybody do come through, it's only gonna be the twins, but they don't usually call or pop up until about nine or ten since they live in Chicago, so we should be good" she said while sitting at the kitchen table.

"So, no ex-boyfriends stopping by?" he asked.

"No, I haven't had a boyfriend in more than a year" she added.

"You mean to tell me with a face like that and a booty that big ain't nobody checking for you?" he complimented her.

"I didn't say they weren't checking, I'm just not accepting, I gotta feel a certain type of way about a person even to date 'em" she continued.

"So, do you feel that type of way about me?" he asked after a brief pause.

"Honestly, I feel something with you, and that's the only reason why you're in my house with dope jeopardizing what I got going on" she spoke honestly.

"Point made" Richie said while nodding his head liking her answers. Then he signaled her to be quiet while pulling out his new cellphone and called JC. Putting the phone on speaker, he sat it on the table. While the phone was ringing, he flipped the bag upside down, and let the five compressed separately wrapped kilos bonded by duct tape fall on the table.

Nita's eyes got wide when she seen all that dope on the table because she had only seen that much dope at one time in movies. She just sat there watching Richie Rich as he examined the work, when JC finally answered. *Who dis?*

"Richie Rich, we met at the club through Quincy" he answered.

Oh yeah, what up? JC asked.

"I'm just calling to let you know that I'm good and I'm getting this shit together as we speak," Richie Rich said. JC could tell that Richie Rich's voice was distorted and seemed distant, so he asked.

You got me on speaker phone? JC asked, only because he didn't know Richie Rich like that and usually when you heard an echo through the phone, it meant you were being recorded.

"Yeah, I got my hands occupied right now, we good though, I'm by myself" Richie continued.

After a long pause, JC asked, *You want me to come through?*

Nita immediately frowned up her face while nodding her head from side to side and mouthing the word 'no'. Richie gestured for her to take it easy, because he had everything under control.

"That ain't necessary, I'm just calling to give you and yo boy a heads up" Richie Rich said.

Well, hit me up when you ready to move, JC replied.

"I'll hit you as soon as I'm done" Richie Rich said before ending the call.

******

"Who was that?" Greg asked with a lit cigarette hanging out of his mouth and an Xbox One joystick in his hand.

"Ol' boy Richie Rich, he said he got that merch from Quincy, and he'll hit us as soon as he whip it" JC said.

"So, what he say?" Greg asked.

"I just told you, nigga, once he put the shit together or do whatever the fuck, he gon' do, he gon' hit us" JC said.

"I'ont like that nigga, Jay, straight up" Greg said after a brief pause.

"Just be cool, we said we here to see that Quincy get them racks back, so that's what we gotta do. All that extra shit you on ain't even necessary" JC replied.

"I'm just speakin' my mind, nigga, if that's alright with you" Greg said.

JC could see that this was taking a turn for the worst, so he just waved him off. "Man, just play that weak azz game" he said.

"Shut yo friendly azz up" he replied.

JC could see that he was not going to leave it alone, so he reached in his pocket, grabbed the pill bottle that was full of Percocets, taking one himself, he passed two to Greg. "Here, nigga, take these and calm the fuck down" he said.

Taking the pills, Greg washed them down with some soda. "Grab the other controller so I can beat yo azz, can't nobody beat me in no NFL Madden and I'll bet whatever" he told JC. "Bet a hunnid" JC said.

"Bet! You ain't seen shit, nigga" Greg added.

"We on, then" JC laughed. "This free money" he added.

******

Stuffing the bricks back in the book bag, Richie Rich threw one over his shoulder and told Nita to grab the other one. Leaving out of the house, they walked down the hallway to the elevator, and rode it to the first floor. Getting to the front door, Richie Rich put the bag in his left hand since his gun was in his right waistband. Going outside, Richie Rich was curious as to where that unmarked police car disappeared to, but more concerned about where them shiesty looking azz niggas were that were posted on the corner. When he seen that the crowd was no longer there, he continued walking to the car pointing for Nita to get in on the driver's side. "Where to?" Nita asked after starting the car.

"We goin' to my crib" Richie said.

"Where's that?" she asked.

"On 39th & Garfield, so just go up North Avenue and make a left on 35th" he instructed her. After getting the location, Nita dropped the gearshift into drive, waited for a car to pass before making a U-turn, and zooming through the intersection right before the light turned red. Nita was trying to make small talk on the way, but she could tell by his one-word answers and head nods that his mind was somewhere else because he kept looking behind them and down every block they passed. She figured he was staying on point in case he seen the police which was understandable due to all the drugs in the car, but all his movements were starting to make her nervous. She was relieved when they finally pulled up in front of his house. Richie Rich grabbed both bags before they hopped out of the car and Nita hit the alarm.

Going inside, Richie headed straight to the kitchen, threw both bags on the floor by the table as Nita walked in and leaned up against the refrigerator.

"Imma be a minute, so you can go in the living room and relax if you want to" he said to her.

"That's alright, I always wanted to see how this was done anyway" she said walking over and having a seat at the table.

"Well, if you gon' be in here, you finna put in some work too" he said, then went straight to work. Pulling out two slabs, he grabbed a hammer, and a small block of wood. Placing the wood on top of one brick, he used the hammer to pound it until it broke apart, then he repeated the same process on the second one. Opening his kitchen cabinet, he pulled out a digital scale, two Pyrex jars, a blender, and a one-pound box of Arm & Hammer baking soda. The way Richie was maneuvering with flawless effort, weighing this, dumping that, whipping up while watching his watch as both Pyrex jars sat in boiling water with the tops covered in plastic made Nita think that was second nature to him as she watched him work. Then she got up, walked to the living room, and sat on the couch once the potent aroma grew too strong.

Richie Rich glanced over his shoulder to catch her leaving, he knew why, but he stayed on his business whipping straight fish scale and bringing back eighteen extra ounces for every two slabs. Now normally you couldn't bring that much back, but the work Quincy distributed came from a Haitian connect in Florida, and he was getting it straight from the boat where it was at least ninety to ninety-five percent pure, so that allowed Richie to maximize what he whipped, so he could maximize his profit. Richie then cooked up two more slabs giving him two extra bricks to work with from the four he whipped up. Richie knew in order to reel 'em in, he had to distribute 'Straight A-1 Drop' the first go round. His mind was already made up that he was gonna bust a couple of 'em down and pump out fat twenties, fifties, and hundreds of that drop until he got Quincy his money, knowing that after that, he was in the home stretch.

After letting it dry, he called Nita back into the kitchen, he sat five boxes of sandwich bags on the table, a box of razors, a box of push pins, two pair of scissors, a couple pair of latex gloves, and put her to work. Opening the refrigerator, he blessed the bottle of Patron Sliver before cracking the cap, taking two large gulps, he sat across from Nita, put the gloves on, and went into bagging up his product. About four hours later, they were finally done, and tired, but Richie Rich knew that time was money and he needed to get in traffic. He decided to give JC and Greg a whole kilo bagged up and a half kilo of crack to serve a little weight with. He'd sell five in weight distribution, and the rest he'd pump however it was ordered. Picking up the phone, he called JC.

"I'm finna get in motion yo way right now" Richie Rich said immediately as soon as he answered.

Aight, I'm waiting on you, JC replied.

"Where am I coming to?" he asked.

24th & Vienna... he said before he was rudely interrupted.

Who the fuck is that?! came loud and clear from the background. JC tried to talk over it, but Richie Rich heard it and knew exactly who it was.

"Tell yo boy Greg to pipe down" he said, trying to keep his focus on the objective and not let it lead him in a different direction.

JC ignored them both before continuing, I'm on 24th &Vienna, it'll be a sunflower yellow Wildcat out front, call me when you pull up, he said.

"Okay, I'll run my plan down to you when I get there" Richie Rich said before another outburst came.

Tell that nigga to hurry the fuck up, he got a nigga waiting on him like we work for him or something, Greg said loud enough for Richie to hear.

"I'll see you in a minute, JC" Richie Rich said before ending the call. He wanted to go in on Greg, but he was not about to be arguing with nobody over the phone, he knew that loud mouthed people had bigger barks than bites, besides, if it came down to it, Richie knew he spoke a different language and he'd let the stick talk if he had to.

******

After the phone call, JC hung up the phone shaking his head. He had only been knowing Greg for eight months, give or take. Greg was originally off of the East Side, he was one of Quincy's baby Mama's little brother, so JC put some trust in him, but he had yet to establish any loyalty to him. JC fully understood his loyalty laid with Quincy and that's why he was there, to assure he'd get his money back, but he had to speak on the situation because it was getting outta hand, and Greg was the reason why.

"Fam, you really trippin' I don't know how this shit even took a turn, but we not here for that, we need to get this money, fuck all that other shit" JC said.

"Man, I ain't tryna hear that shit, fuck dude, my nigga Gunna -rest in peace- stripped the shit outta dude soft azz, you don't even know dude, so why you taking up for him?" Greg said feeling some type of way.

"Come on, fam, I ain't taking up for nobody, the shit just not necessary, we don't need no tension in the air, that shit wit Gunna don't got shit to do wit this, so let's just do what big homie paying us to do" he explained.

"Yeah, whatever" Greg said before turning back to the video game.

******

Richie Rich looked at Nita trying to decide if he should take her with him to drop the work off to JC and Greg. After coming to the conclusion that she already knew a lot, he made up his mind to just roll wit it. He already surprised himself by revealing so much to her so soon, but it was too late for him to be second guessing himself, especially with them trying to start a relationship. He figured that she needed to be battle-tested and street-smart for the line of work that he was in.

"You rollin' wit me, or you want me to drop you off?" he asked, already knowing the answer. Nita looked at her watch like she really had something to do, because although she enjoyed his company, she didn't wanna come across as clingy or a groupie. Nevertheless, she wanted to kick it with him.

"It's only a little after five, so Imma chill with you, if my girls want me, they'll call me" she said.

"Who, dem twins?" he asked.

"Yeah, their names are Tiera and Ciera, we were supposed to be going out tonight" she explained.

"Well, let's hurry up and bust this move then, grab that bag" he said pointing to a small gym bag. "I can't believe you wanna go out when you know you already caught wit me" he joked.

Nita smirked at him, turnt, and started walking towards the door swinging all her hips and ass. "You see all that, don't act like you didn't catch, too" she shot back.

Richie Rich smiled while shaking his head in agreement, she was definitely bad, he loved her sassiness and confidence, it was a major turn-on. Leaving out of the house, they hopped in the car, and before she pulled off. "Listen, we finna go drop this shit off to this one nigga, when we get over here, I'ont want you to say nothin' to these dudes, just stay in the car, and keep it runnin', you hear me?" he ran the rules to her.

"Gotcha" she said while putting her thumb up, but she had no intentions on getting outta the car anyway.

"Don't be offended by what I just said, I'm just tryna look out for you, because when niggas find out that you with me, they gon' be tryin' they hardest to get next to you so they can get next to me, you feel what I'm saying?" he said.

"Yeah, I said I got you" she said after a brief pause, she hadn't realized that until that moment, but she definitely knew that he was right.

"Aight, then, let's roll" he said while leaning back in his seat.

******

"Where my pistol at?" Greg asked JC while looking around for it. The Percs had kicked in and started to affect him.

"It's over there" JC pointed to the speaker. "You ain't gon' need that shit, we know dude ain't on no stick-up shit" he added.

Irritated by what he believed to be JC's passive approach to the situation, Greg voiced his disdain with him. "Let me do me, I was a stick-up kid way before I started husslin, and I don't trust a muthafucka, not you, not Quincy, and certainly not Richie Rich's bitch azz" he said.

"I knew I shouldn't have gave yo paranoid azz that pill, you trippin' already" JC replied as he watched sweat run-down Greg's face.

"Ain't shit about me paranoid, nigga, I'm on point." Greg said grabbing his pistol, ejecting the clip before slamming it back in, chambering a round, and putting it in the small of his back.

Chapter Eight

* * * * *

Making a right on 27th & Vienna, Nita drove down mouthing out the words to 'Not The Only One' by Kevin Gates, until out of the corner of her eye, she seen Richie Rich pull out his F&N, check the chamber, and put it back in his waistband as she pulled up behind the yellow car that Richie Rich said would be on 24th Street. Nita turned the music down and sat quietly because she was terrified of guns and, every time she seen one, her whole demeanor would change. Richie Rich looked to his left making Nita turn to see what he was looking at. There in the doorway stood a 5'10",160-pound light-skinned JC, he had shoulder length dread locks with two tear drops coming down the left side of his eye. When JC stepped on the porch, Greg appeared behind him. Greg was a tall dark-skinned nigga with a bald head, he reminded Richie Rich off of Kevin Garnett. He was leaning against the entrance of the door with his arms crossed tryna look tough while watching Richie Rich get outta the car. "I'll be right back" Richie Rich said. Nita nodded her head trying to look confident, but she wasn't because she had never been in a situation like this before. Her instinct told her something was wrong.

"What up?" Richie Rich said giving JC some dap.

"I'm chillin" he replied before turning to walk towards the house with Richie Rich right behind him. As they entered the door, Greg stepped to the side to let JC walk in. Richie Rich nodded at him and tried to follow JC in, but he was met with a shoulder bump.

"Watch were the fuck you goin', nigga!" Greg yelled.

"Nigga, I'll..." Richie Rich started to say.

"In here bro, fuck what dude talkin' about" said JC.

"Naw, fuck what you talkin' bout!" Greg shouted.

Richie Rich put it in his mind that he was about money, so fuck all the other shit dude was on, but he had to admit that Greg was really testing his patience, and that was making it very hard for him to stay humbled. Walking in the living room, Richie Rich could tell that they weren't trapping outta this house because it was way too clean and had too much furniture. He was so glad that it was only JC and Greg there because he hated doing business with a house full of niggas.

"So, what's the plan?" JC asked as they heard the front door slam and seconds later, Greg walked in and stood against the wall. Uncomfortable with his demeanor, Richie Rich looked over towards him. "What's yo muthafuckin' problem nigga?"

"You my fuckin' problem..." Greg replied.

"Say, man, y'all cut that shit out" JC spoke up trying to keep the peace, but they were already turned up.

"Nigga, I'ont even know you. If it wasn't for Quincy, I wouldn't even be fuckin' wit yo kind" Richie stated.

"Bitch azz nigga, I'ont know you eith..." Greg started to say, but the words were caught in his throat when he seen Richie Rich drop the bag and pull out his F&N.

"You betta watch who you callin' a bitch, cause that don't describe me, I get money and I ain't wit this hoe shit you on, but just because I'ont start problems don't mean I'ont know how to finish 'em" he said before semi turning his head towards JC.

"You seem like a nigga bout his business, so we can do some work, but I ain't fuckin' wit dude" he added when outta his peripheral vision, he peeped Greg reaching for him. Three gunshots echoed throughout the room as Greg slammed up against the wall, slid down it slowly leaving a wide trail of blood, and died right there with his eyes open and his gun in his hand. They say whenever you die with your eyes open, that means you deserved it.

JC jumped back in shock before going into panic. "What the fuck, man? Aww naw... you killed him" he said.

Richie Rich walked over to Greg, bent down, and picked up his pistol. Not sure of what JC was on, he stood up, turned around, and pointed the gun at him while quickly catching a glimpse through the curtains to see if people started coming outside looking suspicious due to hearing the gunshots.

"Whoa, whoa, whoa" JC pleaded with his arms stretched out like he could catch a bullet. "I ain't got shit to do wit you and

dude, you did what you had to do, I'm just here for Quincy"
he continued.

Richie Rich's phone rung, still pointing his gun at JC, he
answered it because he knew it was Nita due to the Beyoncé
song that she programmed her number under. "Hello" he
said.

I heard something that sounded like shots, you alright? she
asked.

"Yeah, I'll be out in a minute" he said before hanging up.

Richie Rich weighed his options, he knew that if both of these
dudes showed up dead, Quincy would assume that he killed
his workers and tried to take his work, so he knew he needed
to keep JC around to confirm his side of the story if it ever
came down to it. Although it was a hard decision, he went
against his better judgement because he knew it was the best
decision, he just hoped the notion didn't come back to bite
him in the ass.

"You comin' wit me, now let's wrap this nigga up" he said.

"Then what, this house in my name, I just can't leave this
nigga here" JC said.

"Exactly, he comin' wit us too, so wrap that nigga up" Richie
Rich said waving his gun back and forth. "I hope you got
insurance, 'cause we finna flame this bitch up" he added.

"What! Hell naw, all my shit up in here, it ain't like they gon'
know he got shot here" JC pleaded.

"This shit ain't open for negotiations, I'm not goin' to jail because what you think they ain't gon' know, you wanna go to jail?" he asked. When JC didn't answer, he said, "Aight then, now hurry up so we can get the fuck up outta here" Richie said then pulled out his phone and called Nita.

You on yo way out? she answered.

"Aye, pull the car around through the alley and pop the trunk" he said then hung up. "Use the rug nigga, damn" he continued after seeing JC looking around frantically for something to wrap Greg's body in.

Tucking his and Greg's pistols in his waistband, Richie helped JC move the coffee table out of the way, and together they dragged Greg's body to the edge of the rug and rolled him up in it. After that, they picked him up and carried him to the back door.

"Hold up" Richie Rich said dropping his end and making his way back into the living room, tossing the book bag back on his shoulder, then used his lighter to set the curtains on fire. Grabbing a T-shirt off the recliner, he stuffed it in between the couch cushions and lit it on fire as well. Running into the kitchen, he stopped, turned on all the burners, and opened the oven before turning it on. Running back to the back door, he peeped out to see if Nita was back there.

"Let's ride" he said lifting his end after seeing she was out there, then they moved quickly towards the alley. Nita sat in the car not knowing what was going on as she watched Richie Rich and some other dude carry a rug to the back of the car and throw it in the trunk.

I know he didn't trade them drugs for that dusty looking azz rug... Nita thought to herself as Richie came around, opened the passenger's door, and tilted the seat forward so that JC could hop in the back. As he hopped in the car, Nita glanced over at him before turning her head back straight forward never acknowledging the dude. She knew something was up and the weirdness of the whole situation had her on edge.

"Go to McGovern Park right quick" Richie Rich told Nita, he decided he'd dump Greg in the small lagoon in the park.

"Aye, pull around the front so I can follow you in my car" JC said.

Richie Rich's mind began to race. Should I let this nigga outta my sight?... I should kill his azz right now, then I'll have to murk her too...fuck! This shit is crazy... he thought to himself while shaking his head from side to side. Sensing Richie's uncertainty, JC spoke up. "Bro, we good man, you got my word on that, I'm just as involved as you" he went on.

"Pull around to the front" he said after a brief pause once he noticed smoke starting to surface from the house, and heard sirens squalling from a distance.

"Somebody must've called dem people" JC said as Nita jetted around to the front.

Pulling up next to the sunflower yellow wildcat convertible, JC jumped out, and got into his car. "Follow us" Richie Rich ordered as Nita smashed off and bent the corner. Looking in his rearview mirror, Richie Rich watched nervously to see if JC was gonna hold true to his word. Seconds later, JC came zooming around the corner behind another car that was behind Richie and Nita. Richie Rich exhaled a sigh of relief, but he knew he wasn't in the clear yet. When Nita turned down 27th Street, she unintentionally caught a little rubber drawing the attention of a squad car on a routine route. Being that they were in a drug infested area, in a fancy car, and the officer couldn't see behind the tints, the officer turned the siren on and pulled them over.

"What the fuck!" Richie Rich said. "Just be cool, you got yo license, right?"

"Yeah" she responded.

"Aight, just don't say slick shit to 'em" he said trying not to panic, but it was hard. He had a brick and a half in the car, two pistols, and a dead body, so he was prepared to hold court in the streets if he had to.

When JC seen them being pulled over, he knew it wouldn't be good, so he kept riding by them. Realizing that he was out for himself, Richie Rich just shook his head in regret, telling himself that he should've killed him when he had the chance. Looking over his shoulder to see what the officer was doing just as he tapped on the driver's side window with his baton.

"Let the window down and turn off the engine, please!" the officer demanded.

"What seems to be the problem, officer?" Nita asked after lowering the window.

"I heard your tires screeching and I thought you may be in trouble, ma'am, and you're coming out of a heavy drug trafficking area with these illegal tints, so you wanna tell me what's going on?" the officer asked leaning down in the window looking at Richie Rich. Richie Rich put his hand closer to his waist prepared to do what he had to do to get himself outta this jam because he could tell the officer was on some bullshit.

"I was visiting some friends over here, I was just..." Nita started, but abruptly stopped when they seen the Wildcat storming down the wrong side of the Street like it was the Indy 500. Coming to a screeching halt causing the officer to jump off to the side. JC lowered his window and yelled "What up, bitch! I fucked yo wife last night, pussy was dry too, I bet you can't catch me" then he burned rubber in place before smashing off.

"This yo lucky day" the officer said before running back to his squad car, hopping in, hitting a U-turn, and speeding after JC. Seconds later Richie Rich's phone rang.

"Yeah" he answered.

Get yo azz up outta there, you owe me one, nigga, JC said then the line went dead.

"Pull off!" Richie Rich said. He smiled not only because he got away, but because JC was who he said he was, and Richie Rich now knew he was 100 and to say he owed him one was an understatement.

******

72

A month later...

"Sir, step out of your vehicle with your hands up... Now walk backwards to the sound of my voice... Stop right there.... Now, get on your knees and cross your feet at the ankles" came roaring from the bullhorn. As soon as he did what was ordered of him, an ATF agent went over and cuffed his hands behind his back.

"Well, well, well, look who we have here. What's up, Mr. Tyrone Q. Miller?" Agent Walsh said while pointing to the K-9-unit officer to take the dog and search the truck. Agent Walsh was a 5'7" 225-pound pear shaped middle-aged white man with a receding hairline. He was the go all out type of cop to get what he or who he wanted.

"You've seemed to have slipped under my radar. You told me that you'd have somebody for me, but I don't see nobody, do you?" Agent Walsh said looking around before pulling out his hankie to wipe the sweat from his forehead. He was so overweight that it didn't take much for him to sweat.

"I'm working on that now, come on man, I told you that. You gotta get me off this highway before somebody see me" he said while looking at all the cars slowing up to see what was going on as the dogs started barking like crazy inside of the truck.

"Well, it seems that's the least of your worries from the sound of it. Let me go see what you tried to slide by me" Walsh said walking to the truck continuing to wipe sweat from his forehead and neck. As Walsh approached the truck, one of the ATF agents had already cut the entire backseat open and started pulling out kilo after kilo.

"Sir, it looks like we have thirty kilos here, plus a bag containing what looks like sixty thousand dollars in counterfeit bills" one of the agents said.

"I know you didn't use that money to buy this" Walsh said pointing to the kilos. "I know it's a bunch of pissed off kingpins waiting to catch up with your black azz" he added, laughing as he walked over to one of the other agents and whispered something in his ear. Once he got the confirmed response, Walsh signaled to the field agent. "Uncuff him" he ordered.

Grabbing Mr. Miller by the collar, Walsh walked back to the truck. "You got three weeks, tops, to get me somebody or I'm locking your black azz up. You can keep the dope, I don't give a shit, you gon' need it to lure me a big fish. However, I can't let you drive away with that money, so you better get a move on it, ole Quincy, ole pal" he continued.

"I got you, man" Quincy said in a pitiful tone.

"Well, get the fuck outta my face and go do your job then!" Walsh barked.

When Quincy looked back towards him, Walsh stood there, shooing him to get in the truck. Walsh peeped his cold stare and knew it was a facade, so he wanted Quincy to know that he was the alpha male and what he says, goes. "If you look at me like that again, I'll make sure that they never find your body" Walsh said loud enough for Quincy to hear.

Quincy didn't say another word, nor did he look back in Walsh's direction. He started his truck and pulled off exiting on the ramp leading to Walnut & Fond du Lac Avenue. Pulling out his phone, he called Greg, and didn't get an answer. Calling JC, he still didn't get an answer.

"Where the fuck could these niggas be?" he said out loud to himself.

Chapter Nine

* * * * *

"Damn bitch, you been actin' funny as hell ever since you been fuckin' wit dude, let me find out" Ciera said with her face frowned up.

"She definitely has been" Tiera added.

"Stop playin', ain't shit changed" Nita smiled.

"Well, why you didn't come to the city wit us?" Ciera inquired.

"Because my man needed my assistance here. I don't have time to just get up and go to Chicago every time y'all want me to" Nita replied.

"Ain't that bout somethin', you hear this, Tiera? That's exactly what I'm talking about, a nigga put you up in a nice azz house out here in Honkeyville, give you a truck, and now you forget where you came from" Ciera said referring to the house they moved to in Wauwatosa and the new Lexus truck Richie bought for Nita.

"You know it's Chi-raq til the death of me, it's where I was born and raised, and when you say truck, make sure you put Lexus in front of it" Nita said.

Tiera was sitting on the couch watching Nita and her sister go back and forth when her eyes drifted to the pair of sparkling heels next to the end table. "Oooh girl, you gotta let me wear these tonight" she said excitedly while jumping up and grabbing them off the floor.

"You gotta be outta yo mind, them red bottoms the real deal and they ain't cheap" Nita spoke.

Tiera looked at Ciera. "So?" she said as she looked back at Nita.

"So?... Them shoes were almost twenty-five hundred and I'm not about to let you stick yo jacked up azz feet in 'em, besides, you wear a whole size bigger than me" Nita argued. "Matter of fact, y'all can have these gold bangles" she added handing them two bracelets apiece. Sliding them on her wrist, Ciera threw her friend a smile. "It's about time you gave us something" she said.

"How much these cost?" Tiera asked being her nosey self while twirling her bracelets around her wrist.

"Don't worry about it, let's get outta here before the club get packed" Nita said grabbing her purse and keys before making her way to the door.

"Where we goin'?" Tiera asked as Nita stopped by the door finishing up her text to Richie Rich letting him know she was on the way to the club.

"We gon' step in Legacy's for a minute, drinks on me" Nita said while locking the door behind them.

"This bitch done got a little money and think she Oprah round this bitch, you get a drink, you get a drink" Ciera said making everybody laugh as they headed to Nita's white Lexus truck.

******

You have a collect call from...

"JC..."

Press five if you... the operator continued before Richie Rich pressed the required button to connect the call. "All calls may be monitored or recorded; you may start your conversation now."

What up, nigga? JC asked.

"Shit, why you ain't call me til now?" he retorted.

I just been goin' through the motions, but everythang good now, he replied.

"So, what they give you?" he asked.

They only gave me thirty days for obstructing, the faggot azz cop said I intervened with his traffic stop, they gave me a speeding ticket too, but Imma pay that when I get released, plus I told they azz I didn't take my medication, JC laughed.

"You need some cash or somethin' cause I'm in traffic now and I'll bring it down there right now" Richie said.

Naw, I get out tomorrow, so Imma need you to come swoop me. The House of Corrections gon' bring me down to the county jail around eight o' clock and they gon' release me at midnight, JC said.

"I'll be there and that was some stand up shit, on life" Richie Rich said.

I hope you would've did the same shit... they both laughed.

"No doubt" Richie continued.

You holla at Quincy? JC asked.

"Hell naw, he said he'd be back in two or three weeks, but it's been a month. I tried to call him, but no answer" Richie added.

He probably somewhere trickin' off wit a bitch, did you put that paper together? JC asked.

"What's my name nigga, I put that up 'bout two weeks after you left" Richie replied.

You have one minute remaining—went the operator.

Well, I'mma get at you tomorrow, turn it up loud when you come through too, JC said letting Richie Rich know he wanted him to bring some kush to smoke on when he came to pick him up.

"I got you" he said ending the call.

******

Richie Rich hung up the phone thinking *perfect timing*. He wanted to ride down and pick JC up in style since he was due to go pick up his new whip from Auto Customizations on South 27th Street tomorrow. He had put his Challenger back in his Aunt's garage after he got it detailed, it was a shame that he ain't even get to really glaze through the city much in the Challenger. He just knew the car would be hot, especially after the stunt JC pulled. Richie Rich couldn't lie; he had surprised himself on how fast he flipped that money for Quincy and got back on his feet. He had been dumpin' weight off to a few of his boys, mainly LJ, JB, and Cuervo left and right. He opened up a spot in Westlawn, Parklawn, and Berryland because he felt like housing projects were able to still be served out of due to how they were set up, and so far, he was right, each house was producing between three and four thousand dollars apiece every day, so he was reestablishing himself back into the game faster and harder than ever before.

The police chief was cracking down on the high-speed chases and drug dealing in Milwaukee by bringing in the Feds. Knowing this, Richie Rich understood that if he was gonna avoid the Feds, his ears had to remain in the streets, he knew the streets always talked and informed one with the information needed. Richie Rich decided to tread lightly even though he had a passion for flashy extravagant cars and jewelry, but he could always explain that because of the insurance money he got when his parents died. Richie Rich hit his signal and switched lanes; he was feeling too good to be back in the swing of things with a whole new sauciness about himself.

Tonight, the city lights were shinning bright, and Richie was another star coming down so fresh and so clean on his way to a club downtown called Legacy to catch up with his boo Nita after she texted him to come through when and if he had some time. Richie was acting out in a black Fear of God tracksuit, fifteen hundred for the jacket and a thousand for the pants. The black-on-black Nike Air Foamposite 1 set his fit off perfectly as he weaved through traffic in the Cutlass on 28-inch Forgiato rims. Adjusting his 'Garfield' chain, he took a few puffs of his Moonrock filled blunt, and turned the volume up to 'Crew' by Gold Link, Brent Faiyaz & Shy Glizzy, and let his subs pound before checking to see what time it was on his Patek.

When he pulled up in front of the club, the line was stretched around the corner, but he knew people with real money weren't standing in no line. Besides, the owner was a close friend of his. Texting Nita, he told her that he was on his way in, then he hit his hazards after double parking, hopped out of the car, walked up to one of the bouncers he knew, handed him the keys and four hundred dollars. "You got this for me?" he asked the bouncer, because Richie didn't wanna go into the parking lot without his pole on him because that was like being a sitting duck during duck hunting season. Without a second thought, the bouncer snatched the money first, then grabbed the keys from him before he opened the door and told Richie to enjoy himself.

When Richie Rich stepped into the packed club, he smiled because it had been a while since he was able to enjoy that type of scenery. Every step he took, he bumped into somebody he knew and hadn't seen in a while. 'It's A Vibe' by 2 Chainz, TY Dolla $ign, Trey Songz and Jhené Aiko thumped so loud through the speakers that Richie Rich couldn't even hear himself talk. Mingling his way through the crowd, Richie Rich made his way to the bar, and signaled for the bartender to come over, once he got done taking care of the customer he was with. Richie Rich smiled at all the attention he was getting; he knew firsthand what Rich Homie Quan was saying a while back when he said he felt like the man when he walked through. Glancing around the club, it was definitely some bad bitches in there in the smallest clothes ever making sure their asses were on display, but there was also a bunch of ugly broads in there too, with makeup caked up on their faces and their hoe helmets sitting on their heads, meaning they had on those cheap wigs and hairdos.

When the bartender finally made it over to Richie Rich, he told him to bring him two bottles of Patron, a bottle of Rosé, and a bottle of Wasted Vodka. As the bartender walked off to go get the bottles he requested, Richie Rich felt somebody tap him on the shoulder. Taking a deep breathe before he turned around because it was an ugly broad at the end of the bar giving him the 'You can get it' eye, and he was hoping she didn't get the wrong impression when he nodded at her, but when he turned around, he was shocked at who he saw.

"Quincy, what's good my dude, why you ain't been answering yo phone?" he yelled over the music.

"I lost that muthafucka while I was outta town, I just got back today" Quincy leaned in and said because of how loud it was.

"I just ain't want you to think that I was tryna play you over that cash cause I got it, and I can drop it off tomorrow if you want me too" Richie replied.

"That'll work...you the last person I expected to see up in here because you always at P. T's strip club" Quincy added.

"I know, but ain't nothing wrong with seeing what the rest of the city has to offer" he said as the bartender arrived with his four bottles. Richie Rich pulled out a fat azz rubber banded bankroll, paid for the bottles while he kept looking around Quincy which caused his paranoia to kick in due to what he was hiding.

"Who you looking for, fam?" he asked.

"My girl, she in here somewhere... she might be over there, take this and let's go check it out" Richie Rich said passing him both bottles of Patron, then leading the way to the back of the club to find Nita. Passing through a crowd of dudes, Richie Rich walked through, but when Quincy tried to walk through, he was met by a shoulder bump that got him heated.

"What up, nigga?" the dude that bumped him said.

"I'ont know you, so what the fuck you mean what up, you bumped me, nigga" Quincy spat ready to square up.

"I know you don't know me, but my cousin know you" the dude said pointing to another dude who was standing off to the side.

"I'ont know that nigga, " Quincy said while looking the other dude over.

"I know, but I seen yo azz earlier" the other guy said.

"Seen me what?" Quincy asked.

"The I-94 ramp, nigga, you know what the fuck I'm talking about" the dude added.

Quincy knew exactly what he was talking about and he wanted no parts of that conversation. He looked to see where Richie Rich was because he certainly didn't want him to hear what the dude was saying. Quincy turned back towards both dudes. "Y'all got me fucked up, I'ont know who the fuck y'all think I am or what the fuck y'all talking about, so miss me wit that hoe shit" he continued as if they had the wrong person, then he walked off as fast as he could while looking over his shoulder to see what the two dudes were up to. Making his way over to a table in the corner where Richie Rich was standing just as a fine super thick chocolate chick got up and kissed him on the lips.

"Hey, bae" Nita said.

"What's good? I see you brought yo lil homies" he said.

"I see you brought yours too, who is that anyway?" Nita retorted because she had never seen Richie with him before.

"This my boy, Quincy. Quincy, this my lady, Nita, and those are her friends, Tiera and Ciera" Richie said.

"What's good, y'all" Quincy said stepping in clear view to peep the two girls out. At first, he didn't notice that they were identical twins, but other than that, they were typical hood bitches to him. He gave them an 8 on his scale, they both stood 5'6" thick as hell, brown skinned with juicy lips. The only difference between them was the thicker one of the two had a mole on her cheek and she wore a mohawk hairstyle, while the other twin wore her hair in a wrap. Quincy tried to turn his sauce up and smoothly nod at them both as he and Richie Rich took a seat at their table.

Ciera squinted her eyes with a curious look on her face as she leaned over and whispered in Nita's ear. Nita's face slightly frowned up, but then she quickly put her poker face back on. Looking over to Tiera for reassurance, the smirk of disgust that was written all over her face told Nita all that she needed to know.

Richie Rich pepped all the whispering, looks, and antics going on and wanted to know what it was all about, so he pulled Nita close to him and whispered in her ear. "What's going on?" he asked her.

Nita was trying to control her eyes and not look at Quincy with a suspicious look, so she stared directly into Richie Rich's eyes and after a quick glance out of her peripheral vision at Quincy to see if he was looking, she mouthed the words *I'll tell you later* to him.

Quincy felt a weird vibe after all the whispering that was going on, but he just thought one of the twins were saying he was ugly or something because he noticed one of them frowning, but he wasn't trippin' about that because he had his money all the way up, and money talked, so if he drove down on one of them, he knew they'd go in a heartbeat, so he ignored the stares momentarily, and hollered at Richie

Rich. "So, what's up with my lil niggas? You heard from 'em?"

"Yeah, JC got locked up for some bullshit, but he get out tomorrow, I ain't heard from or seen that nigga Greg ever since I gave him some work the day after you left town" he said then sipped his bottle.

"Yeah...you know that's my baby mama brother, she said everybody lookin' for that nigga, but he been MIA" Quincy added.

"You know how it be when niggas get some money, he probably out splurging wit a bitch" Richie said.

"On everythang" Quincy agreed. "Imma get on up outta here, hit me tomorrow about that demo when you get out in traffic" he added while looking at the icy Rollie on his wrist, he was starting to feel uncomfortable sitting there receiving awkward looks from the twins. Getting up to leave, he shook Richie Rich's hand, and walked off. As soon as he disappeared into the crowded club, Ciera said, "Girl, that's him on everything" with a stern look on her face.

"You sure?" Nita retorted.

"Hell yeah" Ciera replied.

"Sholl is" Tiera said.

"What the fuck is y'all talking about?" Richie Rich said tired of being in the dark about whatever they were talking about.

Nita put her hand under the table and put it on Richie Rich's knee before she spoke. "Bae, Tiera and Ciera came from the city earlier today and when they passed the ramp on Fond du lac, they saw a black Lac truck pulled over by a bunch of unmarked cars and a K-9 unit, they slowed down to see what was going on..." she said.

"And!" he blurted out wanting her to get to the point.

"One of the police out there was holding up a duct tapped package that looked like dope and the dude Quincy that was just sitting here was handcuffed on the ground talking to a chubby bald-headed man in a suit" she said.

"Now, I ain't a rocket scientist, but if it look like a duck and quack like a duck..." Ciera said.

"Get the fuck outta here, how you know it was dope? Betta yet, him?" he asked, but in the back of his mind, he knew Quincy did just come back in town today because he told him when he first seen him, and how did they know he was driving a Lac truck, a black one at that, it couldn't have been a coincidence.

"You don't have to believe us, but we from the low end of Chicago, so we know what dope looks like, we just tryna help you out, so our girl don't get caught up in none of this mess when the shit hits the fan" Ciera said.

"First off, I got her, she good, know that, so y'all can stay the fuck outta our bidness, and don't be advising her shit" Richie said, scowling.

"Whatever" the twins said in unison.

"I know, whatever" Richie Rich said getting up to leave as Nita stood up. "Look, baby, you ain't got shit to worry about, I promise you that, I'll handle everything, and I'll see you at the house later on, I got something's to take care of, call me when you get to the crib, okay" he reassured her.

"Yeah, you just be careful out there" she said leaning in to kiss his lips.

"You already know" he said looking directly into her eyes before he dug in his pocket, passed her a few hundred, and turned to leave.

Chapter Ten

* * * * *

Around 2:00 am Friday morning...

A light drizzle sprinkled over the city while Quincy drove his Lac truck north on Highway 41 listening to 'No Promises' by A Boogie wit Da Hoodie on his way home, traffic was surprisingly thick considering the time. As soon as he hit his signal to switch lanes, he spotted a familiar looking dark blue Crown Victoria with blue and red lights flashing from within the front grill and the top of the dashboard, so he pulled to the side. Looking in his rearview mirror, he shook his head when he saw Walsh exit his vehicle and make his way to the passenger side of his truck and hop in. Brushing off his coat, he wiped his badge off that hung from the upper left pocket of his coat before he looked over at Quincy.

"I figured I'd pay you a visit to see how things are coming along because the attorney general is on my azz about why I'm letting a piece of shit like you maintain your freedom without any productivity" Walsh said.

"You told me I had three weeks" Quincy replied.

"And you do, but Imma need you to kick it into another gear" Walsh said as he wiped the spit from the corner of both sides of his mouth. "I need this dude like right away" he urged.

"Man, you said—" Quincy started.

"You act like you got a muthafuckin' choice and turn that bull crap azz music down!" Walsh retorted.

"Who you got in mind?" Quincy inquired as he turned the music down after a brief pause.

"Richard Williams" Walsh said.

"Richard Williams, who the fuck is that?" Quincy asked turning to face Walsh.

"You know him as Richie Rich, but we've been watching him for a couple of years now, I just need a little more concrete evidence and then Imma RICO his azz for conspiracy, tax evasion, and whatever else I can put on him, you know when us Feds investigate, we try to put you down for the count" Walsh chuckled.

"I don't know where to find him" Quincy lied.

"Really...that's interesting because I know you were at the club with him earlier, so I know you know exactly where to find him" Walsh replied. His words caught Quincy completely off-guard. It made him realize they had a tail on him. He understood he had to produce, or it was gonna be his azz on the chopping block, but he also wanted Walsh to know it was gonna be hard to do work with his name being thrown around as a snitch.

"Muthafuckas callin' me a snitch because of that stunt you pulled on the freeway..." Quincy told Walsh.

"Well, you are" Walsh interrupted.

"This shit supposed to be on the low, so I can keep my name clean. Niggas find out I'm telling, they gon' try to kill me" Quincy complained.

Walsh wasn't trying to hear none of that, he didn't give a damn if his name got dirty, he put him out there to set people up, so as far as he was concerned, that's what he better be focused on. "Listen, I don't give a shit about that, do your fucking job or Imma lock your azz up for so long that your children's children will have grandkids by the time you get out. Call me when you get something solid" Walsh said while opening up the door, hopping out of the truck, making his way back to his car, and peeling off.

Quincy sat there for a minute weighing the pros and cons to his actions. On one hand, he knew he was about to take a good dude off the streets for a longtime, and then on the other hand, he knew if he didn't, he'd be taken off the streets for a long time.

Knowing all this, he told himself "Fuck it, it's either him or me, and I'll be damned if it's me..." Quincy then turned his music back up and continued on his way home.

******

"What the fuck?! You done snapped the fuck out!" JC yelled ecstatically when he walked out of the county jail and seen

Richie Rich standing next to a four-door sky blue outrageous colored 2014 Mercedes Benz S550 on chrome 26-inch Forgiato rims with the spinning 'F' centerpiece.

"You did that, my dude" he complimented while shaking up with Richie Rich.

"It's been lovely out here, so I had to ride like an athlete because I ball hard, me and money neva been strangers" Richie Rich jacked while reaching in his pocket and pulling out ten Gs.

"That's you, we'll hit the stores up tomorrow and get you together" he added.

"That's love, my dude" JC said accepting the offered money. "So, what's been going on out here? Did you ever get up wit Quincy?" he continued.

"Speaking of that nigga, I heard some foul shit about dude" Richie said.

"What?" JC asked.

"I hear he workin' wit the Feds..." he said.

"Get the fuck outta here!" JC replied, shocked.

"Yeah, my lady lil friends said they seen him stretched out on the highway and dem people was bussin' his shit down, but he ain't get locked up because I seen his azz at the club the same day" Richie added.

"If he workin', why they bussin' his shit down?" JC asked not wanting to believe that the man he looked up to wasn't right. He couldn't believe the man that put him in the position to eat in the streets had turned out to be a rat bastard.

"I'ont know, I was thinkin' the same shit, and what's fucked up about it is I'm tryna look into it but I really don't know where to start, I'ont wanna go around askin' muthafuckas questions and it get back to him. I been fuckin' wit him and I got his cash, but if it turns out that he workin', somethin' gon' have to be done about it, because I'ont know how long it'll be before he tell on me, shit, he fuck around and tell on you too, we'ont know what he gon' be on if he snitchin'" Richie Rich said.

JC knew exactly what Richie Rich was saying, and he knew he was right, so they'd definitely have to cross that bridge when and if they had to. As JC was looking around collecting his thoughts, he peeped something not too far away.

"You see them over there?" he asked while nodding towards the dark colored detect car that was sitting by the corner with three white occupants inside. "And no white dudes came out wit me either, just another black dude, and a Mexican cat, so you know who that is" JC added.

Richie Rich took a quick look over his shoulder. "Yeah, I seen 'em when they pulled up while I was waiting on you, fuck them, but let's get up outta here. The night still young, it's only a little after midnight, so we gon' cruise through the city for a while" Richie said before hopping in the Benz as JC slid into the passenger's seat, he immediately smelled the new car smell as he sat on the plush white leather seats that had 'No

Sky's Are Never Grey' in sky blue letters stitched in the headrests.

Richie Rich definitely out here showing out... JC thought to himself as Richie passed him a blunt of that moonrock.

"Put that in ya system" he smiled while starting the car and turning the volume up a couple of notches to 'Codeine Dreaming' by Kodak Black featuring Lil Wayne. Putting the gearshift into drive, Richie Rich peeled out making a U-turn, and drove up to the corner. When they pulled up next to the detect car, they seen three clean-cut white dudes sitting inside and they thought that they could either be federal or DEA agents.

"Muthafuckas" Richie Rich said under his breath and then turned up Highland Avenue. "Here" he added passing JC his phone. "Call that nigga Quincy and tell me what you think, shit, you been around the nigga longer than I have" he continued.

"Ain't that gon' dirty yo phone up?" JC asked.

"If that nigga snitchin', it won't be long before they know the number anyway. I'll get a new phone tomorrow" Richie replied.

JC took two long pulls of the blunt, then he started dialing the number. "What's good, fool?" JC asked as soon as Quincy answered while signaling for Richie to turn the music down. *Who dis?*

"JC, nigga, why you sound so paranoid and shit?" JC asked.

I ain't paranoid, nigga, a muthafuckas gotta be careful out here. I just don't pick up no phone and start talkin' without knowing who on the other end, besides, I heard you got locked up, Quincy added.

"I did, but I'm out now, what up wit you?" JC asked.

Nothing right now, I'm at the crib. Did you ever get up wit Richie Rich? Quincy pressed.

"I'm wit him now" JC said knowing damn well he seen Richie Rich's number pop up on his screen.

Oh, I was wondering why his number popped up on the screen when you called, Quincy said because he really didn't have anything else to say due to him knowing the Feds had his phone tapped, and with the mere mention of Richie Rich's name, he knew where the direction of the conversation was headed. Truth be told, Quincy really wasn't sold on giving Richie up to the Feds because Richie Rich had a name in the streets, and if it got out that Quincy was snitching, he knew he couldn't get any money in the city and him and his family weren't ever going to be safe. With that in mind, he figured he'd try to incriminate JC, the lowest man in their circle. He thought by giving JC up, Walsh couldn't say he didn't give him somebody.

You know the weather changed, so if you ready to put on them boots on and get a few of 'em, let me know and I got you, Quincy offered.

JC attempted to cover the phone up while whispering Quincy's proposal to Richie Rich, but Quincy heard him.

JC!... JC! Quincy yelled.

"What up?" JC said putting the phone back up to his ear.

Why you discussin' what we talkin' about wit that nigga, my work ain't good enough for you since you been fuckin' wit Richie Rich, he said, putting emphasis on Richie Rich's name. Since he was going to incriminate JC, he figured he'd try to get him to roll over on Richie Rich and make him guilty by association or make it to where JC could possibly get knocked and tell on Richie so he wouldn't have to do it.

"Man, you making a big deal over nothin'" JC said knowing something was up with him.

I'm just sayin', you my lil nigga. Now, I'm picking up my cash from Richie tomorrow, so just let me know, and I got you, Quincy continued.

"Aight, I'll be wit him when he ride down on you, so we'll holla then" JC told him.

Aight, fool, Quincy said.

"Yep" JC said ending the call before passing the phone back to Richie Rich just as he was turning off of Highland onto 35th Street heading towards Vliet, when Richie looked in his rearview mirror and seen the same car that was parked outside of the county jail following them.

As soon as he crossed Vliet, the cops turned their lights and sirens on. "Fuck!" he said pulling over to the right.

"This shit crazy azz fuck!" JC said putting out the blunt, letting down the window, and spraying some air freshener all before the officer made it to the window.

"What seems to be the problem, officer?" Richie Rich said lowering his window after the officer knocked on it.

"It ain't no problem, Richie Rich, I just wanted to see how you were doing" the detective said completely throwing Richie for a loop by calling his name. Then he bent down and sniffed inside of the car. "You done smoking that blunt already, JC? It smelled like some good shit" he continued sarcastically before he chuckled.

"I don't think I know you, so how the fuck you know my name?" Richie Rich questioned not finding the detective's theatrics funny at all.

"Well, it's my job to know the shit I'm not supposed to, and I sure know a lot, trust me" the detective said looking at Richie sternly while moving his head up and down, then he smiled before he continued his shenanigans. "You a ball player? Because this is surely a nice car, I used to date a broad named Mercedes in high school, she slept with my buddy while we were together, and that's where I learned everything that looks good doesn't mean it's good, so I hope you kept the receipt to this bad boy" he smiled. "Now you fellas be safe" he added while tapping on the top of the car, then he walked off, hopped in his car, and pulled off.

JC looked over towards Richie Rich with a stunned expression on his face as Richie Rich turned to face him. "They on us already, that nigga Quincy gotta be snitchin'" he said while dropping the gearshift into drive and pulling into traffic.

"On er'thang" JC agreed.

Chapter Eleven

* * * * *

R ichie Rich and JC walked into the house that Richie shared with Nita a little after 5:00 am in the morning. After directing JC to the spare bedroom, he told him that they'd talk more later in the day, then he made his way to his room, put his phones on the charger, undressed, and hopped in the bed next to Nita. As soon as he pulled the cover up on himself, she turned around catching him off-guard because he expected her to be asleep.

"Where the fuck you been at?" she asked softly, but in an irritated tone.

"JC just got out today so I swooped him up, took him over some chick he know house so he could get himself together, then we went out for some drinks to catch up on a few things. He down in the spare bedroom too, I hope you don't mind, but he needed a place to stay since we burnt his shit up" he explained.

"I'm not trippin' about him, I'm trippin' on why you didn't call me or answer yo phone, you got me around here worried as hell, I didn't know what was going on, especially with what the twins were saying about ol' boy... don't do that to me again" she added before turning back over with her back facing him.

"My fault, baby, my phones died, and we was kickin' it, honestly, I didn't even know it had got that late" he said wrapping his arms around her waist and pulling her naked body towards him until his manhood was pressed against her butt.

"Who was over that girl house for you?" she shot.

"Stop it, you know it ain't that type of party, my baby right here" he said while becoming erect from grinding on her butt.

"Whatever move" she said acting like she didn't want him up on her.

"Don't act like that, baby" he said placing kisses on her neck behind her ear which was her spot.

"Move, boy... mmm" she said and when Richie Rich heard her moan, he knew he had her, so his small kisses became wet sloppy before he started sucking on her neck while he maneuvered his finger in between her legs, into her moist vagina, and fingered her while sucking on her spot which caused her to go into a frenzy.

"Ooooh, baby…" she moaned.

Richie Rich rolled her over, got on top of her, and started sucking on her breasts. Nita reached down, grabbed his member, rubbed it through her plump labia until the head was moist from her juices, then she guided him inside of her.

"Aaaah" she moaned as she spread her legs wider to receive his total length after she adjusted to his strokes. Richie Rich long dicked her until her scratches on his back became too much to handle, then he pulled out, flipped her over into the doggystyle position, spread her ample ass cheeks, and slid into her from the back.

"Awww, Richie…" she said after he slapped her ass hard, then he held her ass and drove deep causing Nita to try and run. She moved her left knee forward and Richie followed suit, then she moved the right one and he followed that one as well never missing a beat. Nita repeated this process until there was nowhere else to run. Richie slowed his strokes but made sure it was a forceful impact after each stroke, then he spread her cheeks and spit on her ass hole. Using his index finger, he moistened her 'glory' hole, and as he slid his finger in, he picked his pace back up and took the day's stress out inside of her.

"Ooooh shit… Aaah baby, I'm finna cum…" she screamed as Richie Rich felt his own climax nearing which caused him to pump even faster while continuing to move his finger in her butt and using his other hand to smack her ass.

"I'm cummin', daddy! Ooooh, Richie!" she screamed as she coated his dick with her juices, and he erupted deep inside of her at the same time.

"Fuck" Richie said before he pulled out and laid next to her spent.

"You missed me, huh?" Nita smiled while getting closer to him to lay on his chest.

"Why you say that?" he asked.

"Because that's how you just fucked me" she replied.

"I always miss you and this" he said squeezing her ass.

"If you come in this house again at five in the morning, you won't get it again" she laughed.

"Yeah, okay" he said then kissed her forehead before he went to sleep. Unbeknownst to him, Nita wasn't going to sleep just yet, she fucked him real good, so that he could go to sleep, so she could get his fingerprint and get into his phone so she could do some investigating. It's not that she didn't trust him, but she had been hurt before. She wanted to see what he was up to, and if nothing, she'd make it up to him, but she had to know to be at ease.

******

Richie Rich opened his eyes to the sun glaring in them and a warm sensation on his lower region. He reached down and grabbed the back of Nita's head and guided her until she slapped his hand away, letting him know that she had everything under control. Richie watched as she deep throated him with no hands and pulled back squeezing with her lips and letting her tongue roll around his shaft. Then she cuffed his balls between her thumb and index finger and pushed them upwards before she slid back down into the deep throat. Once at the base, she opened her mouth wider, stuck her tongue out and licked his balls while his dick was in her throat. Richie loved that trick, then she slid back up slowly while making eye contact with him to see if he was enjoying what she was doing to him. Getting to the top, she pulled it out, slapped it against her tongue three times and then gave him some fast head.

"Damn, baby... shit" Richie said. "Aww, it's cummin', baby" he added in a low growl as he shot his load in three squirts into her mouth. Nita continued sucking allowing him to finish, then she pulled him outta her mouth, kissed the tip, and swallowed his baby-making protein batch.

"I'll be in the shower waiting on you" she said after getting up, then she walked off naked with ass and titties bouncing everywhere.

Nita knew what she wouldn't do, another woman would, so she put it down every single time she fucked him or sucked his dick, so her man had no reason to cheat on her. Besides, Nita had an auntie that was five years older than her, and schooled Nita on everything growing up, and she told Nita that when she was coming up, she'd suck her man up every morning, and she called it sucking the hunt out of him, because if he was on empty before leaving the house, the chances of him trying to release somewhere else were slim to none. He was her man, and it was her duty to please him just as it was for him to please her, and she always remembered that, so once they moved in together, she surprised him the next morning with some head, and every morning after that. Needless to say, she didn't find anything on that phone, or he would've been burnt up on her morning rituals.

Richie got outta bed smiling, ever since he and Nita moved in together, she had woken him up with some head to start the day every single day, and he couldn't get enough of that.

Nita fully understood what it was to be a man's woman, she fed him and made sure his balls stayed empty, and he did everything he could to keep her happy and smiling, they had a great relationship thus far. Grabbing a towel, Richie made his way to the bathroom, brushed his teeth, and then hopped in the shower with Nita. After going at it for about thirty minutes or so making sure each other was pleased, they exited the shower and went to the bedroom. Richie oiled her down in massage fashion, then he handled his hygiene, and went to his closet.

He put on his blue jean Balmain jeans with the knee out, his navy-blue leather Louis Vuitton loafers with no socks, his navy-blue Louis Vuitton tight fitting t-shirt, and navy-blue Louis Vuitton belt with the big 'LV' buckle. Brushing his hair, he then put his gold and thirty pointer diamond Cartier glasses on, his gold Rolex, and his gold and diamond chain with no charm, then he stuffed twenty Gs in his pocket. Looking himself over in the mirror, he knew he was styling and profiling.

"Baby shoot this video for me" he said while handing her one of his phones and stuffing the other one in his pocket, then he stood in front of his shoe rack which had over a hundred pairs of shoes on it.

"Go ahead, baby" Nita said as she aimed his phone.

"It's that nigga Richie Rich again, y'all know why they call me that, I'm finna get in traffic, but Imma up you up on my apparel first, eleven hundred for the shoes, twelve hundred for the pants, six hundred for the shirt, eight hundred for the belt, six Gs for the Cartier, and I'm rockin' plain Jane, but it's still seventeen Gs for the Rollie and you know the saucy drippin', just so I don't gotta look like you fuck niggas when I step out. A light twenty grand to blow in the store today that I'm driving to in big boy S550 Benz of Forgi's, I ain't gotta tell you what that cost, but it separates the niggas who really gettin' to the bag from those pretending, I do what I do cause most niggas can't, know that..." he said and signaled for Nita to stop recording.

"You is crazy" Nita said shaking her head and laughing. "I hope you not about to post that?" she added.

"Imma post it to my Insta later on, not before I get in traffic, but I gotta let it be known that I'm back in full effect" he said.

"If you say so" she said before he left to go see if JC was up yet.

Walking to the guest room, he opened the door, and saw the bed made up and JC nowhere in sight. Going in the living room, he found JC sitting on the couch watching an old DVD of now Notre Dame standout Arike Ogunbowale and her high school, Devine Holy Savior Angels up state were Arike set the state record of fifty-five points in a single tournament game while eating a bowl of Fruity Pebbles.

"I see you up early" Richie Rich said sitting on the other couch.

"I was hungry as a bitch, I came and made a bowl of cereal, then I seen you had this DVD wit Arike on it, she probably the best girl to come outta Wisconsin with Shemera Williams right behind her" JC said.

"You shoulda woke me up if you was hungry" Richie replied.

"I figured you needed all your rest after last night" JC added.

"After we left the bar?" Richie asked.

"Naw, nigga, after what was going on in that room last night. It sounded like you was killing her, literally... oooh, Richie..." JC laughed.

"You stupid" Richie said joining in on the laughter before leaning back and putting his feet up on the coffee table while turning to his thoughts.

"What's on yo mind?" JC asked after seeing Richie was focused.

"Check it out" he said after a brief pause. "The move you pulled at yo crib let me know that you a standup dude and believe me when I say I'm thanking you every day for it because that. Shit could've gone totally different, but what I'm 'bout to run by you is as serious as it gets, and I need to know your take on it. I know we ain't been fuckin' wit each other that long, but with me seeing that you'll go to great lengths without a second thought let me know you valid, so Imma trust you with this info" he continued.

"Aight, bro, I'm wit you on whatever it is, real recognize real, and just to put everything on the wood, the nigga Greg was acting like that because he said you got into it with his guy Gunna or some shit like that a while back" JC went on.

Richie Rich was taken back by the information that JC just revealed to him, now he knew why Greg was acting like a bitch. As far as he was concerned, they could continue to be guys in hell. He just had no idea that dude knew of his past, but Richie maintained the determined look on his face and never commented on that information.

"Aye, it's all good, but like I was saying. I know how this shit goes, if these muthafuckas watching us and following a nigga all around town, then this shit is getting serious, and if that nigga Quincy is working with dem people, at some point he gonna have to give a nigga up and testify against us, you feel me?" Richie said. JC nodded knowing Richie Rich's analysis of the situation was indeed accurate.

"That nigga gon' have to have his trial" Richie said.

"What you mean?" JC inquired.

"You know, death" Richie replied, sounding calm.

"It's whatever bro, I ain't finna let that nigga take me down, but what you gon' do about the work you be getting from him and his money too?" JC asked.

"Fuck that nigga work, we can take his shit after we cancel his snitchin' azz, niggas like him need to be put in a concrete slab" Richie Rich said just as Nita walked into the living room.

"You hungry, baby?" she asked.

"Naw, I'm good" he answered.

"Well, I wanted to let you know that Tiera and Ciera are on their way back up here from the Chi to pick me up, Imma go there to visit my auntie because she's sick" Nita said.

"That's cool, when you coming back?" Richie inquired.

"I'm only staying for a few days" she informed him.

"Aight, that'll give me some time to handle some things in the streets, you need some money?" he asked.

"No, I'm straight" she assured him.

"Aight, let me finish hollering at JC, then I'mma come holla at you" Richie said.

"Okay" Nita said before walking off into the kitchen to let him continue his conversation. Her intuition told her that he was up to no good and she hoped that he would be safe and stay out of trouble while she was gone.

"So, what you think about that?" Richie Rich said once Nita was out of earshot.

"I'm wit it, but where?" JC asked.

"I don't know yet, but I'll have it figured out before the day is over, but in the meantime, let's hit the mall and spend a little money" Richie said.

"Hell yeah, wearing these clothes I went to jail in got me feeling wrong, I need to get fresh ASAP." JC said rubbing his hands together.

"Nita!" Richie Rich yelled.

"What, baby?" she asked coming from the kitchen eating a fruit salad.

"We finna go do some shopping, you coming?" he said already knowing in his head the answer to that question.

"Yeah bae, let me grab my purse" she said before heading back into the kitchen.

"Where we goin'?" JC asked.

"We gon' hit up Icons on the South Side, then shoot out to Mayfair" Richie added.

"Cool" JC said.

"I'm ready" Nita said coming from the back holding her phone looking too cute in a pair of tight-fitting Saint Laurent jeans that hugged her ass, matching tight baby tee that had her breasts sitting up and showed off her pieced navel and flat stomach. A pair of 3-inch open heel and toe Saint Laurent sandals complemented her look; her taste was nothing short of impeccable, she looked so good to Richie he gave her the once over.

"You look good, baby" he said leaning in to kiss her.

"Thank you, baby, so do you" she said after she kissed him.

"You driving, too" he said handing her the keys to the Benz while she walked out the door, he stood there admiring her ass and that bad azz walk that she had that got him every time. Richie shook his head, set the alarm, and then headed out to the car.

"Walsh speaking" he said answering his ringing phone.

Aye, I got something you may be interested in… Quincy said.

"It better be someone and not something" Walsh replied.

Imma get you JC first, and I'm supposed to be picking up two hundred and fifty thousand from Richie Rich later today, Quincy said.

"I hope that money is from the investigation" Walsh pressed on.

Yeah, Quincy replied.

"Well, that's good, but you gotta come up with more concrete evidence than that, the system won't hold him long enough just for that money, I wanna nail his azz to the cross. So just in case I wasn't clear enough, fuck JC, he isn't my target, he's a peon in the operation, get me Richie Rich or you'll be the one behind bars, and you better hurry because I got people watching him now, so if they get him before you do, then you still go to jail" Walsh said then hung up on him.

******

Walking out of the mall with five bags apiece in their hands, about six thousand lighter, and after blowing thousands in Icons, they walked through Mayfair mall's parking lot. Richie spotted a white dude sitting in a car with a white woman, and they looked to be engaged in a conversation, but he could've sworn he seen the man lowering a camera out of view when he looked in their direction. Either they were the Feds, or he was just paranoid, whatever the case, he lowered his head and sped up to his car because he didn't wanna alert Nita of this and have her scared, but he knew that he had to hurry up and do Quincy before he did him. Getting in the Benz after putting the bags in the trunk, Nita sped off going North on Mayfair Road. Richie Rich looked back to see if the car that occupied the white couple was following them, seeing they weren't, he looked towards JC. "We doin' that shit tonight" Richie said.

"I'm wit you, bro" JC said. "Aye, Nita, can you stop at the gas station on Capital so I can get me a pack of squares" he continued.

"Okay" she answered.

"I just hope you know you ain't about to be smoking no stankin' azz squares in this car" Richie Rich said.

"I already know, but I still need 'em" he laughed.

"You need to quit smokin' that bullshit anyway, my nigga" Richie Rich said before he turned to talk to Nita.

******

Where are you? Walsh asked.

"I'm sitting at the gas station on Mayfair Road & Capital where I told you I was gon' be, where you at?" Quincy asked.

Imma block away, I'll be pulling up in a minute, and this better be good, Walsh said.

"Yeah, it's good alright, Imma get Richie Rich azz for you" Quincy said.

That's my boy, I'll see you in a minute, Walsh said ending the call.

******

Richie Rich was talking to Nita about not going to Chicago running her mouth and discussing his business about what he had going on with her family members while JC was in the backseat looking through his bags trying to figure out what fit he was gonna put on when he went to see one of his baddest hoes. He certainly needed to get his dreads twisted up and get a taper fade as well. He wanted to go back and holla at her tonight after that GAP she put on him last night after he got outta jail, her ass was so phat, and her head was so good that he had yet to stop thinking about her, but he knew he wasn't gonna see her because Richie wanted to go push Quincy's shit back tonight, but she was definitely on his to-do list for the next day. Nita was coming up on the gas station when an old white lady threw on her signal and veered in front of them making them miss the turn into the gas station.

"What the fuck is this old bitch doin'? I know she betta have some insurance if she hit my shit" Richie Rich pissed off.

"Don't say that, that's somebody's mama" Nita said.

"It ain't mine" he replied.

"Dawg, look at that shit, don't turn around Nita, keep goin'!" JC said enthusiastically.

Richie Rich turned and looked "What the fuck!" he said. As they drove past the gas station, they saw Quincy getting into the front seat of an unmarked police car with a white man. "Let me see yo phone, I'm finna call this nigga and see what the fuck he gon' say" JC said reaching for the phone Richie was handing him. "Don't say nothing" he added as he dialed the number and put the phone on speaker so Richie Rich could hear.

Hello, Quincy answered.

"What up, nigga?" JC asked.

JC? Quincy said catching his voice.

"Yeah, what up?" JC continued.

Shit, what you on? Quincy asked.

"Down here in the hood, come slide on me, and fuck wit ya boy" JC added.

You wit Richie Rich? Quincy asked.

"Naw, I ain't seen him since yesterday, why? Where you at?" JC asked, again.

I'm at my OG crib eatin', so I'll catch up wit you later, Imma bring you something through there when I ride through, Quincy said.

"Bring me something? I ain't ask you for shit, I just said come fuck wit me" JC said not trying to incriminate himself. "Who you wit, why it sound like a white dude there?" he added knowing damn well he didn't hear anything in the background, he just wanted to see how Quincy was going to react.

Wh—what? You trippin', you might've heard one of my lil nephews' bad asses runnin' round here yellin', but I'll catch up wit you later, I gotta take care of somethin', Quincy replied.

"Yeah, whatever" JC said ending the call and passing the phone back to Richie Rich. Leaning back in his seat, JC just stared out of the window shaking his head in disbelief until he broke the silence. "That shit crazy as fuck!"

"I told you nigga, shit gotta be done tonight" Richie Rich said before turning towards Nita. "Baby, Imma need to take a rain check on this shopping trip, but I promise that we'll do it as soon as you get back from Chicago, okay?"

"Okay, you want me to drive back to the house?" she asked.

"Yeah, baby" he said loving her understanding ways, then he leaned back in his seat while plotting his next move. The entire ride back to Richie and Nita's house, JC was fuming from Quincy's deception because he was acting like he was a standup guy when all along he was a rat bastard. A rat who just lied to him like he was a peon when he had just seen him getting in the car with that cop. JC was really fucked up behind what he saw, but he wasn't as furious as Richie Rich was, because he knew it was only a matter of time before the

Feds came kicking down his door if he didn't make Quincy disappear. When Nita pulled up in front of the house, Richie Rich hopped out of the passenger's side, and walked around to open the door for her.

"Baby, grab that thang out the stove in the grease catcher for me" he said.

"I got you" she said while grabbing her bags, then she walked off as JC got in the front seat of the Benz.

A couple of minutes later, Nita returned, kissed him passionately on the lips while passing him the towel in her hand. Nita used to be terrified of guns, but Richie had them all through the house, so she had gotten a little comfortable with them. "I love you" she told him.

"I love you, too" he said gripping two handfuls of her voluminous ass after he placed the towel on the seat. "Call me when you get to Chicago and don't forget what I said." he added while digging in his pocket and handing her a couple thousand dollars.

"Thank you, baby, be careful, and I didn't forget, but I wasn't gonna do that anyway, I know how it goes" she smiled as she put the money away before pecking him on the lips one more time.

"Turn the alarm on before you leave and put yo truck in the garage" Richie Rich said getting behind the wheel of his car.

"Alright, see you later, baby" she said waving as she sashayed back into the house.

"You will" he smiled while thinking that he should run in the house and hit that one more time because he couldn't get enough of that ass, but he changed his mind because if he didn't handle the business at hand, he would probably never be able to hit that again. Unwrapping the towel, he pulled the .40 caliber and the 30-round clip out, stuffing the clip in the gun, he pulled the hack back to chamber a round, then he sat it on the seat, and pulled off from his house.

"You got any ideas on how you wanna handle this?" Richie Rich asked as he turned off of the block they lived on.

"Yeah, let's take the nigga in the basement of an abandoned building, torture him, take his work, and bury his azz alive with the maggots. I seen that shit on CSI Miami when I was in the House of Corrections" JC said.

"That's actually somethin' to think about, but I think we should cut his azz into pieces and put him all over the city. Better yet, let's do somethin' mob worthy and cut his fuckin' head off" Richie Rich said.

"On everythang, that's the move" JC said liking the idea. "Go by my grandpops crib on 24th & Burleigh, he got a shack in the back, I'm sure it's an axe in there, rope, and some other shit we may need, but we gotta find a way to get him to come up off some of that dope" JC continued.

"I got it, I know exactly how we gon' do this. I'm gon' have to sacrifice one of my spots, but it'll be worth it in the end" he said pulling out his phone.

"Who you callin'?" JC asked.

"Quincy, watch this" Richie instructed.

What up, fool? Quincy answered recognizing the number.

"Shit, I'm on my way back to the town from the Chi, I had some business to take care of, but I'm tryna meet you tonight to drop that cash off to you and I'm gon' need to snatch a few white bitches, too" he said speaking in code letting him know he wanted some kilos.

How much? Quincy asked

"Salt buck if you toss five and get it on the bizzack" Richie asked.

I see you on that, huh? Quincy added.

"Somethin' like that, I ain't out here for nothing. Just get that together and I'll call you later to let you know where I'm gon' be at" Richie added.

Aight, in a minute, Quincy said.

"Yep" Richie Rich said ending the call. Then he called one of his lil guys who he had working the sack for him.

Who dis? Trell answered.

"Rich, nigga" Richie said.

Oh, what's hat-nen my dude? Trell asked.

"Get everythang up out that house and wipe everythang down. Nobody is to be in that house no more, it's officially shut down, but don't trip, Imma get you another one soon, aight?" Richie continued.

Got you, Trell responded.

"I need you to get me a joint too" Richie added.

A pole? Trell asked.

"Naw, a whip, and park it in the back of the crib" Richie responded.

Keys or it don't matter? Trell asked, following.

"Don't matter" Richie replied.

I got you, Trell reassured him.

"Do it ASAP, my nigga. I got you and bust every streetlight on the block too and be discreet both ways" Richie instructed.

Aight, I got you, I'll hit you tomorrow, Trell replied.

"No doubt" Richie said ending the call as they were pulling up in front of JC's grandparents' house.

JC and Richie were both excited to get back at Quincy for the bullshit that he was doing when he thought nobody knew, but they both knew his time on earth was quickly coming to an end.

"You ready to go get the shit?" Richie asked.

"Let's go" he said as they got out of the car and went to the small shed. When they returned, they had an axe, rope, duct tape, and a box of rat poison that JC found in the corner of the shed. He figured if Quincy wanted to be a rat, he might as well eat what they eat and die.

"Let's make this shit happen" JC said feeling betrayed as he closed the trunk after loading everything in it.

"Definitely, I like that in you. Most niggas know one of they niggas snitchin', but they still fuck wit 'em sayin' or rather thinking that the nigga wouldn't tell on them, but I'm not gon' even give a nigga a chance to snitch on me. If a nigga the police, he betta get the fuck from round me before my trigger finger starts itching" Richie Rich said as they hopped in the car. He turned up 'How It Feel' by Money Man and rapped a part of it.

Heard you gettin' money, how it feel nigga

I heard you gettin' money, how it feel nigga

Bitch, I rock a chain like a field, nigga

how the fuck you real

and you squeal nigga…

Richie rapped feeling the lyrics and knowing what had to be done as he pulled off.

Chapter Twelve

* * * * *

T he sun started to disappear behind the clouds as the night grew near. The city awakened to participate in the night life activities that Milwaukee had in store. Although Richie Rich wanted to indulge, he had other objectives that he needed to handle first. Quincy had to be taken out before Richie Rich found himself sitting in a federal courtroom with Quincy as the lead witness in his indictment which could potentially have him staring at a one-way ticket to a life sentence behind the walls of Levingsworth Federal Penitentiary, or any federal joint for that matter, point being, he wasn't about to go out like that. Looking at his Rollie, it was that time, so Richie pulled out his phone, and dialed Quincy's number.

What's good, Richie, where I'm meeting you at? Quincy answered.

"Meet me at my crib on 39th & Clark, it's a white house next to the only brown one on the block, you can't miss it" Richie said.

You there now? Quincy asked.

"Yeah, I'm waitin' on you if you comin' now cause I got a move I gotta make tonight" Richie replied.

I got you, I'll be there in fifteen minutes, Quincy said.

"Aight" Richie added.

Yep, Quincy said, ending the call. Quincy was trying to stall until he got in contact with Walsh, so he could put a car on him to verify the transaction, but Walsh hadn't called or answered his phone since earlier today, so he'd just have to take his word when he said he delivered the work to Richie Rich.

******

When Richie Rich hung up, he explained to JC to pull his Benz into the alley next to the stolen car which was a newer Hyundai Accent, then he told him to come into the house after he did that. JC agreed, hopped in the driver's seat, and pulled off. Richie went into the house and went straight for the backdoor to unlock it for JC. He could tell his lil guys did exactly what he told them to do because there was nothing left in the house but the furniture and appliances. Making his way into the living room, he took a seat on the couch while looking around trying to see where he was going to position himself when Quincy walked in. He couldn't believe that he had found himself in the position of having to body yet another nigga so soon, but he had to. He understood that the game he was in was a marathon, and that you had to eliminate your competition by distributing the highest quality product, having a complete whip game, utilizing your ingenuity skills better than the next man, and the number one rule was to never snitch on anybody. Knowing all of this, Richie Rich knew the only way he could maintain his freedom and continue to stack his money up was by taking Quincy out of the game.

"So, we gon' do the shit here?" JC asked while entering the living room snapping Richie out of his thoughts.

"Naw, we gon' take him on 38th to this abandoned house" Richie answered.

"38th and what?" JC asked.

"Between Lloyd and Garfield" Richie Rich said getting up to peek out of the window.

"Aight" JC said sitting on the couch. "I can't believe this hoe azz nigga tellin'." he added.

"Yeah, it's fucked up, but it was the same way when everybody knew Alpo was tellin' Nicky Barnes, Frank Lucas, Nino Brown, the square azz nigga Q.Z., the nigga Rio who told on Boss, you remember that, big-mouthed Scooby wit his soft azz, and that punk azz bitch Tye. Some muthafuckas you just don't understand it from when they supposed to fuck wit you, like why you wanna see me suffer if you fuck wit me, niggas just don't be built for the shit they be tryna do out here, but fuck 'em" Richie Rich said.

"I feel that" JC said as the room fell silent for a couple of minutes.

"Where the fuck this nigga at?" Richie said checking the time on his watch. "I'm finna call him now" he continued while pulling out his iPhone. Just as he was dialing the number, an incoming call came through. "This him right here...hello" he added answering the phone.

Imma be pulling up in about two minutes, Quincy said.

"I'll be on the porch" Richie said ending the call. He thought about sending JC outside to meet Quincy because he didn't know if Quincy had the Feds on his tail or not, and Richie didn't want them taking any surveillance photos of him, so that's why he had his lil guy Trell bust every streetlight outside. Richie was really hoping that Quincy wasn't that far into it, to where he was an option to be told on, so that was why he made the decision to do it now rather than wait for the shit to hit the fan. After a brief debate with himself about what he was going to do, he decided to go because Quincy didn't know JC was with him and he didn't want him to start getting suspicious, he needed him to be relaxed, and thinking this was going to be a quick transaction. Richie Rich ran the plan down to JC about what he was supposed to do, then he peeked out of the window to see a black Lac truck creeping up the street.

"There he go, get on point" Richie said while pulling his snap back down low on his head before walking out of the door and closing it behind him. Walking on the porch, Richie Rich looked down the block both ways for any suspicious cars or people as Quincy hopped out of his truck and walked up carrying a duffel bag. Richie Rich wanted to pull his .40 out and leave his fat azz stankin' right there on the pavement by that dog doo doo for that shit he was trying to pull, but he knew to succeed in the game of power, you had to master your emotions, so he showed some self-control.

"What's good, Richie?" Quincy said walking up with his hand extended.

"Chillin', bro" he said shaking his hand and one arm hugging him, but while he was doing that, on the sly Richie brushed up against him to see if he was strapped and he could tell that he had somethin' fat in his waistband.

JC stood looking out of the window watching everything that was going on until he seen Richie Rich give the signal that Quincy was strapped, and they were on their way in. JC knew that if the hit to the head didn't knock Quincy down and they were unable to get to his waist before he did, that he'd have to pop Quincy and he had no problem doing that as he went and took his position behind the door.

"Come on, let's go in the crib and handle this so I can go bust this move before it get too late and then get up wit these bitches" Richie Rich said turning to walk up the steps.

"Fo' sho... Aye, what up wit one of them thick azz twins that yo girl be kickin' it wit?" he asked while following him.

"Oh yeah, the one that's a little thicker said she like you too, that's what the whispering was about at the club, she be actin' shy and shit, you know how bitches be, but Imma plug you wit her" Richie Rich said thinking to himself that the only way he'd see her again was in heaven or hell.

"On what she at me?" Quincy asked.

"On everythang" Richie answered.

"Yeah, hook that up for me, my dude" Quincy added.

"I got you" Richie said opening the door and walking in the house. Once Quincy walked in, JC hit him in the back of the head with the butt of the gun as hard as he could.

"Fuck!" Quincy yelled as he fell to the floor. Richie Rich quickly turned him over and pulled his gun from his waistband and his cellphone from his pocket. Then he held him down and let JC put the zip ties on Quincy's hands.

"Now turn yo bitch azz over before I blow yo shit all over these walls" Richie Rich said while pointing his pistol at him as JC snatched the duffel bag off the floor.

"You niggas stick up kids now?" Quincy said after he turned over.

"Shut yo snitchin' azz up" Richie said.

"Snitch! Nigga, I ain't no muthafuckin' sni—" he tried to convince them before JC cut him off.

"Nigga, we seen yo police azz at the gas station wit that fat azz white detective, who was that, the Feds? Or was that yo mama because when I called you, you said you was at yo mama house, remember that? So, tell me, when did yo mama become a white man that live on Mayfair Road, huh? Or was that one of your bad azz nephews runnin' around?" JC said revealing they knew of his deception. Quincy knew that he was cold-busted, and he was unable to come up with the right words to say because he knew that he was bogus.

"Get yo bitch azz up" JC said helping him to his feet.

"Man, y'all can have all that shit, the dope, the money, whatever. I ain't gon' say shit I promise just let me go" Quincy tried to bargain after not having anything else to say.

"Shut that stupid azz shit up" Richie Rich said slapping him across the face with his gun causing him to spit up blood after he stumbled backwards a few steps. "Is them bitches out there waiting on us?" he continued.

"Naw, I swear to God" Quincy pleaded.

"Good, tape this bitch azz nigga's mouth closed" Richie barked as JC pulled out the roll of duct tape and taped Quincy's mouth shut. As soon as he was done, Richie grabbed Quincy by the back of his shirt, pressed the gun to his back, and led him through the kitchen to the back door.

"When we get outside don't get stupid and make me have to shoot you, because I certainly won't hesitate to, and I hope you wouldn't try me and find out, we clear on that?" Richie said as Quincy nodded his head, then Richie and JC led him out of the backdoor into the alley where JC opened the trunk to the Hyundai.

"Unt uh" Quincy mumbled shaking his head knowing that shit was about to get real.

"Fuck you mean unt uh, you gettin' you bitch azz in there" JC said while dropping the duffel bag, then he hit Quincy with a barrage of punches causing him to lean over by the trunk, then JC and Richie scooped him up, and threw him in the trunk before slamming it shut.

Richie Rich looked at JC and was impressed at how personal he was taking the situation, fully understanding niggas like Quincy is the reason the game was so fucked up now. He was glad to see someone besides himself invested in making sure this snitch understood the consequences of his actions, but this was merely nothing compared to what they had in store for him. Richie Rich then pulled out his cellphone and made a call as he walked back into the house.

Everything good, my dude? Trell answered.

"Yeah, good looking, my dude, but I need one more favor" Richie said.

Shoot, Trell replied.

"Aye, it's a black Lac car parked in front of the spot, the keys on the kitchen counter, I need it to disappear like yesterday. Don't play with this my nigga, do it now, and I got something for you, no bullshit" Richie instructed.

Aight, I'm finna go do it now, Trell responded.

"Good lookin,' my nigga, love" Richie said.

Love, Trell said ending the call as Richie came back outside after putting Quincy's keys on the counter.

"Drive to 38th Street in between Lloyd and Garfield and pull up in the alley. Imma follow you, but take the side streets" Richie Rich said.

"Aight" JC said accepting the key to the Hyundai, hopping in, he started it up. He could hear Quincy mumbling in the trunk as he backed out from the side of the garage.

"Shut yo bitch azz up before I start shooting through the seat" he continued, and the mumbling stopped. He smiled as he looked in the rearview mirror to see Richie Rich pulling up behind him, then he smashed off to their destination.

******

Walsh sat in his car checking the messages on his cellphone. He received several phone calls from Quincy, but he was unable to answer them because his phone was off due to him being at his granddaughter's recital. He knew today was the day that Quincy was supposed to go meet up with Richie Rich and deliver the kilos, but he hoped like hell that Quincy didn't go alone. He knew he should've put a wire on him, but he knew when people wore a wire, they unconsciously acted a little strange trying to get as much information as they possibly could, and a seasoned hustler like Richie Rich would've scoped that out and blew his case up, so he didn't do it. He tried calling Quincy several times, but there was no answer.

"Shit!" Walsh said while banging his hand against the steering wheel because he felt that Quincy was about to blow his case. The plan was to have Quincy deliver the fifteen kilos to Richie Rich, then as soon as the transaction was made, he'd have the Feds run in the house and haul everybody to jail. He knew that would be sufficient enough in federal court so that Richie Rich would never see the streets again, along with the surveillance photos of him making drug transactions with other people throughout the city. Walsh found it odd that Quincy wasn't answering his phone especially after he threatened to lock him up with some of the same guys he helped get off of the streets, and that led him to believe that Quincy did something stupid. After dialing his number a few more times to no avail, he hung up, called one of his operatives, and told him to put a trace on Quincy's phone.

Chapter Thirteen

* * * * *

J C pulled into the alley on 38th Street pulled to the side so that Richie could take the lead since he didn't know what house they were going to. Richie Rich drove halfway down, hit his lights, and pulled up as close as he possibly could to the abandoned house. Hopping out of his Benz, he signaled for JC to wait as he went around the house to kick the backdoor in. Coming back to the back of the house, he waved his hand for JC to come on before he grabbed the sack with the tool handles poking out of it from the trunk and slung it over his shoulder. Closing his trunk, he walked over to JC who was standing at the back of the Hyundai holding a .9 mm in his hand ready to open the trunk. "Get his bitch azz outta there" Richie said after looking around to see if anybody was watching them.

JC opened the trunk and said." Let's go nigga" seeing a slight hesitation, he reached in, grabbed him around the neck with his left hand, and slapped him with gun that was in his right hand. "I said now nigga" he barked in a low growl. As Quincy started to get out, JC yanked him the rest of the way out causing him to hit the ground with a thump. Quincy let out a muffled moan through his taped mouth as Richie Rich and

JC picked him up and started walking him to the house. Quincy knew something terrible was going to happen to him if he went into that house, so he tried to take off running, but the strength of two men pushing him into the door was too much for him considering that his hands were tied behind his back.

"Get yo bitch azz down there" Richie Rich said as he and JC violently pushed him down the basement stairs. Unable to use his hands to break his fall, Quincy's head touched almost every step as he tumbled down the stairs. He winced in pain as he laid in the fetal position until the pain subsided. Richie Rich made sure the door was secure, turned on the light, then he and JC walked down the steps. They each grabbed one of Quincy's legs and dragged him to the middle of the floor where Richie Rich dropped the sack of tools on the moldy wet concrete basement floor. Then he wasted no time as he put on his baseball gloves, went over and landed some powerful punches to Quincy's ribs breaking two of them in the process before he ripped the tape off of his mouth. Quincy growled out in pain.

"That ain't shit nigga, after today you won't ever get a chance to snitch on another muthafucka" Richie Rich said.

"I... ain't... snitch on... no muthafucka, y'all got the game fucked up..." Quincy explained between coughs.

"Ain't shit else to talk about" Richie told him as he grabbed the sack and dumped all the tools out.

Quincy didn't know what to expect when he saw Richie Rich fumbling with the tools. Having no other way to protect himself, he rolled over, and raised his legs up into the fetal position.

"Turn yo azz over!" Richie Rich barked, but Quincy didn't respond or turn over. Before Richie could go over there and make him turn over, JC took care of that. Quincy yelled when the bullet from JC's .9mm penetrated and ripped through his calf muscle. "Now roll yo bitch azz over" JC said.

"Shut yo azz up, duct tape that nigga's mouth back closed" Richie said as JC pulled out the tape and did what Richie asked of him. "You thought you was gon' sacrifice me, so you can have longevity in these streets? Yo hoe azz was sadly mistaken because I ain't finna let that happen" he continued while staring down at him in pure pity.

As JC started to rant towards Quincy, Richie Rich bent down, and picked up a hammer with his gloved hand. Quincy completely disregarded what JC was saying as he saw Richie Rich walking over to him with a hammer in his hand. His eyes grew wide when he saw him cock the hammer back and come crashing it down against his ribs breaking a few of them. One of his broken ribs pierced his lungs and made it very hard for him to breathe. Quincy rolled back and forth with tears coming out of his eyes in sheer pain. He mumbled something and Richie struck him again, this time in the chest. The pain was so unbearable that Quincy wished that they would just kill him and not make him suffer. "Imma make the last three minutes of yo life a living hell, you snitchin' bitch" Richie Rich promised.

Quincy laid there with tears streaming down his closed eyes wondering how he found himself in a position like this, because this was definitely not a part of the plan. His breathing began to get deeper because of his punctured lung as he laid there knowing his fate was death.

"Imma show this nigga what disloyalty brings you" JC said sliding into his one-piece mechanic jumpsuit and putting on a pair or work goggles. "Once I separate this nigga head from his body, Imma call up my bitch, get some pussy, and sleep like a baby" he continued while picking up the axe and tossing it over his shoulder before going to stand next to Richie.

"You did this shit to your muthafuckin' self, I never played you or did you dirty. Even if I did, that don't make it right for you to tell on a muthafucka, now don't it?" Richie Rich asked but Quincy didn't respond.

"You heard him, muthafucka!" JC said raising the axe and bringing it down into Quincy's leg. Quincy let out the most horrifying muffled scream that JC had ever heard in his life.

"Don't cry now, nigga!" Richie Rich said before kicking him across the face, then he bent down and ripped the tape from his mouth.

"I'm sorry man...I fucked up" he said gasping for air as he started sobbing and whimpering.

JC dug back in the sack and pulled out a small box the size of a baking soda box.

"Open yo muthafuckin' mouth, you wanna be a rat, then eat this rat poison" JC was about to pour the small, poisoned pellets into his mouth until Richie Rich stopped him.

"Hold up, I got a better idea" Richie Rich said after seeing something moving along side of the wall. "Help me catch this" he told JC, after helping him out, JC watched what Richie Rich did next before he re taped Quincy's mouth. That was something that he hadn't even seen in movies before. "Gon' head" he added.

JC picked the axe up. "Damn you, Quincy..." JC said as Quincy looked up at him, his life flashed before his eyes, then all he could see was darkness as JC brought the axe down on his neck. Quincy's head rolled off to the side as his body went into convulsions for about one minute, then it went limp.

"Finish choppin' that nigga up while I put his head in this bag" Richie Rich said while using a towel to wipe the blood off, then he duct taped the bottom of the head before putting it in a black garbage bag, and taping that closed. "When we dump his azz, Imma throw his phone in their wit him, so when they find him, they gon' find his muthafuckin' head disconnected from his muthafuckin' body" he continued.

"Hell yeah" JC said before lowering his goggles back over his eyes and continuing to dismember Quincy's body.

Richie Rich watched on until Quincy was completely mangled and dismembered. The only thing that remained was his torso. "That's all I can do, we gon' have to leave this part like it is" JC said, covered in blood. "We burying his azz anyway so it don't matter" he added while looking down at his clothes. "I gotta get outta this bloody azz shit" he continued.

"Throw that nigga body in a bag and triple it up so we can get the fuck up outta here" Richie Rich said handing JC the bags as he dashed out to the car. While Richie Rich left, JC stuffed Quincy's body into the garbage bags, and tripled it. Just as he was tying the bag, Richie Rich came back with a big gas can, a towel, and a pair of shoes for JC.

"Here" he said passing JC the towel and shoes. While JC got dressed, Richie doused the entire basement in gasoline, even the mechanic suit and shoes JC wore. Grabbing Quincy's head and body, they walked up the stairs with Richie Rich leaving a gasoline trail up to the backdoor. After setting flame to the gas and making sure it went to the basement, they crept out of the abandoned house with Richie Rich holding the bag that contained the head and JC holding the body. Tossing the body in the trunk of the Hyundai, Richie Rich put Quincy's head on the passenger's seat of his Benz.

"Aye, follow me" Richie yelled in a whisper before he hopped in his truck and started it up. The night skies camouflaged their need to be inconspicuous as they pulled out of the alley, drove a block over, made a left on 37th Street, drove down, made a right, and traveled east bound on North Avenue trying to obey the speed limit so they wouldn't draw any unnecessary attention to themselves even though Richie Rich was driving a Benz on 26-inch chrome Forgiato rims.

Richie Rich glanced up into his rearview mirror to see if JC was still behind him, but the glare from the headlights behind him made it hard to see, so he weaved through traffic and looked back to see a car doing the same things, so he figured that had to be JC. Pulling up to the lights on Teutonia & North Avenue, Richie Rich made a left turn to go towards

Keefe Street just before a couple of oncoming cars passed which caused JC to have to wait. The third car coming from the opposite direction made a right and JC shook his head in disbelief when he realized it was a squad car. However, JC made the turn to get behind the police car that was now directly behind Richie Rich's car and kept a little distance between him and the cop car.

Being able to spot a cop car from a mile away was survival skills 101 in the ghetto, so when Richie Rich directed his eyes back into his review mirror, he immediately knew that he was in front of a police car. Slowing down his speed slightly so they wouldn't have a reason to sweat him because everything else was good. *If they stop me, should I show them my license and hope for the best? What if the Feds looking for me? Damn, I got this nigga head sitting on my passenger's seat, fuck! If they pull me over Imma stop and when they get out I'm pulling the fuck off, if that don't work I'm holding court in the street...* Richie Rich wrestled back and forth with his thoughts as he reached for his .40 caliber and put it on his lap.

They followed Richie Rich until he pulled up to the lights on Center Street, then they swerved and pulled up on the passenger side of his car to have a look at the driver. Although he didn't want to, Richie Rich looked to his right, locked eyes with the cop, smiled, and nodded his head to the lone officer. The officer nodded back at him then turned down Center Street. Richie Rich let out a long sigh of relief as he looked down at Quincy's head that rested in plastic on his passenger's seat. JC saw the squad car turn off and let out an equally long sigh of relief as he pulled up on the passenger's side of Richie Rich signaling for him to lower his window.

"Where we goin'?" JC asked.

"Just follow me" Richie Rich said letting his window back up and pulling off just as the light turned green. Driving up Teutonia until he came up on Keefe Street, then he made a left and drove up to 20th Street turning into the cemetery right before he made it to the lights. JC followed close behind and now understood why they traveled across town once their destination was revealed. Richie Rich drove about fifty yards deep into the cemetery, pulled over, turned his lights out, but kept the engine running as he stepped out and grabbed the shovel from the backseat. However, he left the head still sitting in the passenger's seat. JC hit his lights, stepped out, opened the trunk, and grabbed the bag that contained Quincy's body.

"We gon' put his bitch azz over here" Richie Rich said pointing before walking over by a three-foot tombstone where he started digging until there was a large two-foot hole. "Throw him on in there" he added just as his phone rung. JC tossed the bag in the hole then stood there and waited while Richie Rich answered his phone.

Hello? Richie answered.

Hey baby, I'm just calling to let you know that I made it here safely, Nita said.

"Aight, baby, but Imma need to call you back in a little while because I'm a little busy right now" he said.

It betta not be with no female, I know that, she said with sass in her tone.

"Stop it" he said.

I know, I'm just playin', but call me back, I love you, Nita said.

"I love you, too" he said ending the call before putting his phone back into his pocket.

Pulling out Quincy's phone, Richie Rich strolled through his outgoing call log and noticed that he dialed a certain number numerous times and it had a weird area code, so Richie Rich pressed send on that number. When he heard a white man's voice screaming through the phone about Quincy's whereabouts, Richie Rich tossed the phone in the hole with the body and covered it with dirt until it was filled back like it was, then he patted it down with the back of the shovel to make sure it was smooth.

******

"Hello... Hello! Why the fuck are you calling me only not to say anything?" Walsh screamed through the phone. "You better have that information for me by tomorrow or I'm putting your azz in jail, you hear me? Huh?" he added before hanging up.

******

Richie Rich and JC got back into their cars and pulled out of the cemetery. Driving a decent distance from the cemetery, they turned into an alley and parked the car. Richie Rich pulled out his cellphone and called his lil guy Trell.

It's done, Trell answered.

"Good lookin' my nigga, but I need you one more time, and I swear Imma get you extra together tomorrow" Richie said.

What you need my nigga, I got you, you already know that, Trell said.

"My nigga" Richie smiled. "I need you to come and get that demo that you gave me earlier and destroy that muthafucka too" he added.

Got you, where it's at? Trell added.

Richie Rich gave him the details about where he could find the car and told him that the key would be under the driver's side mat. He also reminded him not to be on no bullshit, do what he told him to ASAP and Trell fully understood what he was saying.

"Aight, love lil bro" Richie said.

Love, Trell said ending the call.

After wiping the car down, Richie Rich hopped into the driver's seat, and JC into the passenger's side seat after he tossed the head in the back seat to get it away from him as Richie Rich smashed off heading in the downtown direction.

Chapter Fourteen

* * * * *

Richie Rich made it downtown a little after 11:00 pm, traffic was mild considering it was downtown. As he drove, the city lights reflected off of the glossy paint that was on the Mercedes. Riding down Wisconsin Avenue, he passed the Riverside Theater and pulled up to the lights on Water Street. JC had no idea of their destination and he didn't ask, he just sat back deep in thought as the light turned green.Richie Rich drove up the small hill until he reached Jackson Street, then he turned right. "Hand me that head" he told JC.

JC reached in the backseat, grabbed the head, and handed it to Richie Rich who was already lowering his window. Grabbing the head, he slowed down slightly and tossed it out of the window towards the parking meters on the other side of the street, then he smashed through the lights, and hopped on the freeway. "Why you throw it right there?" JC asked.

"It's the federal courthouse building, where they bring muthafuckas like me to defend myself against police azz niggas like him. We did them a favor and dropped their lead witness back off to them, now he can still be their head witness, ya feel me?" Richie Rich said with a devious smile as him and JC shook up.

******

"Did you run a trace on that number like I asked you to?" Walsh asked one of his operatives.

Yes, sir, I did. The signal is located on 20th Street, somewhere off of Keefe Street, one operative said.

"What's there?" Walsh asked.

A cemetery from what I see, it's smack dead in the middle, he continued.

"A cemetery?" Walsh replied curiously. "I'll be back... keep the trace going on that phone and let me know if that position changes" he added as he grabbed his holstered service weapon.

Will do, sir, he said.

******

"You think we good now?" JC asked Richie Rich after accepting the blunt of kush.

"We should be, we got a quarter mill, fifteen bricks, and everything else that we already had" he responded.

"I ain't talkin' bout that, I'm talkin' about wit the Feds?" JC asked.

"They just lost their lead witness, I don't know what else they got, but you would think we'd be good, but it's too close to call right now" Richie Rich said receiving the blunt back and taking a few pulls on it.

"We out here then" JC said.

"On er'thang, we finna go stupid hard on they dumb azz" Richie Rich said as the Benz disappeared into the night.

******

Thirty minutes later...

"Hello?" Walsh answered.

Sir, we have a big problem... Agent Santos said.

"I'm at the cemetery now, where is he?" Walsh asked.

I don't know, it's still reading that he's there, but he's also here... Agent Santos replied, nonplussed.

"What? What do you mean he's there?" Walsh barked.

Sir, they found his head... Just his head in a bag outside of our building. We took it out and heard something squeaking in his mouth, so we removed the tape to find a live rat inside of his mouth... Santos said as the line went silent. Sir, are you still there? Santos added.

"Yeah, I'm here" Walsh said dryly. "Send me a team down here, I take it that since his head is there, then his body is probably somewhere in the cemetery... And give me Richard Williams' number, it should be highlighted next to his picture on the board in my office" Walsh instructed. After getting the number, Walsh ended the call, then called Richie Rich.

Hello? Richie Rich answered.

"That won't help your case" Walsh snarled.

What the fuck is you talkin' about? Better yet, who the fuck is this? Richie asked.

"I think you know" Walsh replied, seething.

I'ont know what the fuck you talkin' about, Richie added.

"I guess you figured out that he was going to give you up, so you killed my witness, but this is far from over, I'm not going to rest until your azz is put away for the rest of your life" Walsh said angrily.

Is that a threat? Richie taunted him.

"Take it whatever way you want to, but I'm going to get you" Walsh promised himself.

Yeah aight, until then, Richie Rich said smiling as he hung up on him.

Chapter Fifteen

* * * * *

The next day...

BREAKING NEWS flashed across the screen before the news anchorperson briefed the public on the latest homicide in the concrete jungle, better known as Milwaukee. Then he introduced the field news reporter who was live on the scene where the grewsome homicide took place earlier. "Thanks, Bill, I'm here at the cemetery on North 20th and Keefe Street where local police assist the US Marshals in digging up a person's decapitated body. It has been reported the person was killed not long ago and buried in this cemetery behind me" the reporter said as the cameraman zoomed in on all the police moving about behind the yellow tape taking pictures and looking for evidence. "It is unclear which part of the body that has been decapitated, the gender of this person, and how they got here. The US Marshals are supposed to be briefing us first thing in the morning, and they do have a person of interest...I'm Shauntel Binns reporting live on TMJ 4, back to you Bill" the attractive reporter with the nice pair lips said as the screen switched back to the anchorperson behind the desk at the studio.

"You see this shit?" JC commented.

"I'm watching the same shit you are, so of course I see it" Richie Rich replied, annoyed.

"Damn, my nigga, what the fuck wrong with you?" JC asked.

"Did you hear what she said? She said the US Marshals got a person of interest, who the fuck you think they talkin' about?" Richie Rich said just tryna get some shit off of his chest. "Then this fag called my phone talkin' bout he gon' get me and shit, we covered all our bases, so it ain't no way they can lead this shit back to me, they probably only looking for me, because they didn't say people of interest" he added while scratching his chin.

Richie Rich knew it was only a matter of time before they came and scooped him up. He didn't believe they had anything concrete on him, at least not enough to charge him with murder, and without Quincy, there was certainly not enough evidence to RICO ACT him on any drug charges, but Richie Rich knew that you could never be too sure of what they knew as he begin to retract in his head all of his steps, to make sure that he didn't leave any loose ends untied. He sat deep in thought until JC calling him snapped him outta his zone. "Did you hear me?" JC asked.

"Naw, what you say?" Richie responded.

"I said what you wanted me to do for you?" JC continued.

"I need you to drop that brick and these few gees off to my lil nigga Trell, he came through for me hard when I needed him" Richie added.

"Where he at?" JC asked him.

"Imma have him meet you at my crib on 39ᵗʰ and Garfield, he straight, so it ain't shit to worry about. After we dump the rest of this work, Imma call my nigga Ant up and have him plug us, he 100, I was just fuckin' wit Quincy cause his prices were a little cheaper, but now we know why. But I'm tryna run it up before they come snatch me up, feel me?" Richie said.

"I feel you" JC said knowing everything that Richie said was highly plausible. "I know a few people who gon' wanna cop a few of 'em, so Imma make some calls and get 'em gone" he added.

"Here go the key to my crib, you already know where we put that shit at last night, I already texted Trell number to yo phone, he know what's up so call whenever" Richie said.

"I got you, what you finna do thou? I know you ain't finna stay in this house hiding out and shit, we straight, nigga" JC said.

"Hell naw, I'm out here in the Benz wit plenty bands in my pockets, Nita supposed to be back tonight, the twins coming wit her too, so we gon' step out tonight, I gotta keep living how I been living to keep suspicion down, you rolling?" Richie asked.

"Hell yeah, I'm finna hit lil buddy up, handle that, then Imma go over my sister crib, get some rest or something." JC said while sitting on the recliner and lighting up a cigarette. "What's them twins name?" he added.

"Tiera and Ciera, they from Chicago" Richie Rich said as he went into the bathroom.

"How they look, they bad, they strapped?" JC asked, curious.

"They straight, and they definitely thick" Richie replied.

******

"Is everybody in position?" Walsh asked through the small microphone that was secured against his wrist.

"We are sir, on your cue" one of the agents said.

******

"Say, bro, I'm finna jump in traffic and go take care of that, then Imma go get me some rest, them Imma get dressed and call you when I'm on my way!" JC yelled down the hallway where the bathroom was.

"Aight, bet! Lock that door when you ride out" Richie yelled back.

"I got you!" JC said then he left the house, but not before he locked the door. Walking to his grey Buick Lacrosse, with the black leather seats and tinted windows, he hit the alarm. As he approached his luxury sports car, he noticed a suspicious looking black dude staring in his direction, but he disregarded it when he seen him pull out a set of keys from his pocket and hit the button disarming the alarm on his own car, then he got in, and pulled off.

******

Sir, do you want us to take him? one of the field agents radioed in and Walsh listened.

"Negative, do not engage...I repeat... Do not engage, he is not the subject, let him go" Walsh ordered as he watched JC drive off. Silence surrounded Richie Rich's home as the agents surrounded his perimeter. The sun was beaming down quite hard this particular day as everyone radioed in that the exits were secured. Walsh made his way to the forefront with two agents carrying a battering ram, crept up to the front door. Walsh silently counted to three, then he yelled in a commanding voice. "MOVE! MOVE! MOVE!" Walsh yelled.

Chapter Sixteen

* * * * *

Richie Rich was beyond pissed as he sat in an enclosed room with a steel table and two chairs, the typical arrangements of an interrogation room. He knew why he was there, because Walsh made it perfectly clear when he hauled him out of his home in only a pair of basketball shorts, no shirt, but they did allow him to put on a pair of shoes and Richie slid into his retro #7 Barcelona Olympic Air Jordans with the number 9 on the back of them. The room didn't have the traditional two-way mirror, but there was a surveillance camera mounted in the corner of the wall to record all interrogations for legal reasons and proof of confessions without force or coercion. Richie Rich had been sitting in that room for 45minutes, but to him it felt like he had been in there for hours. As he leaned back staring at the ceiling, he started to tap his feet, and bob his head to 'Blog' by Moneybagg Yo. Standing up, he leaned against the wall with his arms crossed when the door flung open, and in walked Walsh accompanied by US Marshal Ms. Gomez who was just transferred to the eastern district of Wisconsin.

"Sit your azz down" Walsh ordered to Richie Rich, but he didn't budge, so Walsh walked over to him with that same tough man posture that all law enforcement used and stared up at him. "You think you're tough, don't you? Well, listen here, Richie Rich... Richard Williams... Brick man... Boss man...scum off the bottom of my shoe. You fuckin' with the big boys now, this ain't state, so sit yo azz down like I told you to" Walsh barked.

"Listen here, man!" Richie Rich said before getting off the wall and standing firm with his fists semi clinched. "I don't—"

"Don't come at me with all that rah rah shit you muthafuckas talk, sit down!" Walsh said while pointing to the chair that was positioned at the end of a small steel table.

Shaking his head, Richie Rich pulled the chair out from the table with his foot and sat sideways in the chair facing Ms. Gomez who didn't blink or show any signs of being intimidated. She just came from the West Coast, so Richie Rich's little antics didn't impress her nor deter her approach and it showed when she opened her mouth. "Mr. Williams, we have word to believe that you murdered and decapitated Mr. Miller, and I would like to know your take on that" Gomez said.

"Am I under arrest?" Richie asked.

"No, you're not, but from what I have here" Gomez replied while going through a stack of papers. "You were the last one to seen with Valerie Storm, and we also believe you had something to do with the murder of Tammy Smith... umm, you may know her as Bubbles, but the big thing here is that is wrecking our brains is the same bullets that were used to kill Ms. Storm are an exact match to the bullets that were used to kill Mr. Demos, otherwise known as your best friend Chauncey, so we believe you also had something to do with that murder as well, and it was a grewsome one, I know you know, you were there, right?"

"What the fuck is you talkin' about? I don't even know a Valerie, a Tammy, Mr. Miller, or what the fuck you talking about for that matter, and why would I kill my best friend? That was my brother, so I don't even know why you would insinuate some shit like that, ain't that some state shit anyway, why y'all fuckin' wit me?" Richie asked.

"Bullshit, you know exactly what we're talking about" Walsh said as he walked over and sat down making his presence felt. "See, what makes this a Federal case is that you killed a Federal witness who coincidentally was gonna inform on you" he added.

"Y'all got the wrong guy." Richie said putting his hands in the air.

"Listen, we been watching Mr. Miller, Quincy, as you know him for years now, around the same time we started watching you, your brother RJ, Jamillah, Chauncey, and the whole little clique, but fortunately for you, they died, you got shot, hence killing our investigation and our indictment dreams. Now you're back balling, and everything has come full circle. We caught your boy, Quincy, with a couple kilos, and he decided to work in effort to keep his azz out of jail, so that's how he got down with us" Walsh explained. As he was talking, Richie recognized that he was the cop that they saw Quincy getting in the car with on Mayfair Road.

"Man, save that shit, y'all just can't come snatch a muthafucka up with no evidence, no witnesses, or none of that shit. I heard about how you bogus azz muthafuckas be doin' muthafuckas... I wanna talk to my lawyer" Richie Rich said.

"You think we stupid or something, huh?" Walsh started to say before he was cut short by Gomez when she nodded towards the camera.

"Fine, we'll question you when your attorney is present, until then, you're being detained" Gomez added.

"For what?" Richie asked.

"I just told you why, since you know the law so well, then you know that we have seventy-two hours" she smiled.

Richie Rich sighed in disbelief, Richie knew that he needed to call JC because he had kept it 100 since he met him, he really didn't have any family that he fucked with like that besides Jacoby and he was too young. He thought about calling Nita, but she wouldn't be back until tonight and he didn't wanna scare her and have her speeding back to Milwaukee and something happens to her, furthermore, he didn't wanna involve her and put that much weight on her shoulders so soon, so JC had to come through for him because he needed him to handle some business ASAP. "Let me get my phone call then" he said.

"You want your call now?" Gomez asked.

"Yeah, let me get that call" he said knowing that without a doubt they were gonna be listening in on his conversation waiting on any inclination of a conspiracy. He was so glad that he gave JC one of his phones because before they could go to the cellphone shop to get him a new phone, they ended up seeing Quincy getting in the car with agent Walsh on Mayfair Road, so they never made it there. Walsh walked over and assisted Richie Rich up by his arm and walked out of the door with Gomez close behind. As Walsh guided Richie Rich to the phone mounted to the wall, he made sure that Richie knew and understood that they were on top of their game as well, leaning over he whispered. "Who you calling, James Cooper, oh yeah, my fault, yo boy JC? That was nice of you to pick him up from jail, and give him that money, you are a semi good guy" he smiled.

Richie didn't acknowledge what he said, instead he threw him a side stare mug. "You sholl do play a lot of games to be a federal agent, more than I would ever care to, now if you don't mind, I'm tryna make a call here" he said while turning, picking up the receiver to the pay phone and using his shirt to wipe the earpiece and the mouthpiece before he put it to his ear as Walsh stared at him menacingly. Richie then turned around. "Can I get some space, so I can make my call, damn" he added.

"Let's give him a little privacy" Gomez said while slightly tugging on Walsh's shirt as they walked down the hall just enough to be out of earshot.

When Richie Rich saw that they were posted down the hall, he started to dial the numbers. "Fuck" Richie said as the answering machine picked up, he decided to leave a voicemail to let JC know what was going on. "Bro this me, these muthafuckas ran in the crib and got me, talkin' bout suspicion of murder, but they lyin' like a muthafucka, Imma try to call back later so when you see this number pop up again, answer it my nigga. Look in the phone, text Nita and let her know what's up, don't forget my nigga, love" Richie Rich said before hanging up the phone. Turning around, he started walking towards agent Walsh and Gomez, who resembled a younger version Rosie Perez, with her little cute mouse face. "I need to try back later because nobody answered" Richie said.

"That won't be a problem" Gomez said as Walsh opened the door to a small cell that had a bench secured to the wall, and a metal toilet that had a sink connected to it.

"A big baller like yourself can't even get somebody to answer the phone for him with as much money as you got... we'll wait til you get to the Feds, you'll have to get a kitchen job just to make ends meet, and that girl you got is gonna run off with JC and have his baby while spending your money, just ponder that for a minute, but for now, welcome home" Walsh said throwing his final jabs at him before slamming the door.

"Man, fuck yo Archie Bunker lookin' azz." Richie Rich said through the door as Walsh walked off.

Chapter Seventeen

* * * * *

The next day...

"Wake up, JC... I gotta go home and get dressed so I can make it to work on time, you seen my keys?" Miranda asked while stepping into her thong before sliding her skirt on. JC opened his eyes and wiped them with the back of his hand. "Yo keys over there by the TV, baby" he said while sitting up in his bed after he stretched. "Make sure you hit me when you get off work tonight" he added while watching her get dressed, then he smacked her on the ass.

"Boy, stop, and I am going to call you" she smiled. Miranda was a pretty caramel-skinned woman that JC liked a lot, they were dating, but not quite exclusive at the moment, but he truly enjoyed her bedroom skills as often as he could. Grabbing her keys, she kissed him, and left out of the door. JC flipped the covers on his bed back, slid out of it, and put some shorts on his naked body. Then he made his way to the bathroom to brush his teeth, take a piss, and wash last night's sex session off of him in the shower.

Fifteen minutes later, he was out of the shower drying off before wrapping the towel around his body and making his way back to his bedroom at his sister's house. Sure, she was family and he loved her, but it wasn't nothing like having your own shit. The insurance company was set to go out and investigate the fire at his house and if they didn't find him liable, they were going to cash him out the sixty-five thousand the house was worth, plus his belongings inside, so he couldn't lose either way, he still had the money and kilos that him and Richie Rich busted down from Quincy, so he'd be looking for a new place very soon. Putting on his boxers and socks, he put some deodorant and powder on before looking through the bags that he bought yesterday at Icons on the South Side. Sliding his tan Ferragamo pants on, he put his white, red, and black stripped three button Ferragamo polo shirt on, and his white, red, and black low top Ferragamo sneakers. Pulling his dreads into a ponytail, he tied a rubber band around them, and sprayed on some Polo black fragrance. "The bitches love the smell of this" he smiled while looking himself over in the mirror, then he sat on the bed to gather his thoughts. Lighting a cigarette and taking a few puffs, he picked up his phone realizing he had a missed call, and voicemail. Pressing the icon button to hear the voicemail, he put the phone to his ear:

Bro this me, these muthafuckas ran in the crib and got me, talkin' bout suspicion of murder, but they lying like a muthafucka, Imma try to call back later so when you see this number pop up again, answer it my nigga. Look in the phone, text Nita and let her know what's up, don't forget my nigga, love.

"Aw naw, you gotta be fuckin' kidding me" JC said while pulling the phone from his ear and staring at it after hearing what Richie Rich just said, he still couldn't believe it.

Putting his cigarette in the ashtray, all he could do was shake his head as he laid back on the bed motionlessly with his eyes closed and his arms stretched out still clutching the phone in his hand. Still trying to process his next move, he already knew he was gonna help Richie Rich out any way he could. Thorough niggas were hard to find, and JC knew if he was in Richie's position, he would want somebody to take care of a few things for him as well. JC knew he had to inform Nita as Richie asked him to. Sitting up, he strolled through the stored numbers until he seen her name then he pressed the call button unsure of just how he was gonna break the news to her.

After two rings, Nita answered the phone and immediately started going off thinking it was Richie Rich. JC just sat there holding the phone letting her get it off of her chest. He knew how a woman could get when they felt threatened as if another woman was possibly snatching the attention away from them. Anytime a man didn't answer his phone for his woman, nine times outta ten she would think that he was fuckin' off on her, a woman's intuition is dear to her, but not 100% accurate all the time. Sensing she wasn't gonna stop, he spoke up. "Nita, this JC" he said.

Oh, where Richie at? she asked after a brief pause, she was slightly embarrassed.

"They got him" JC added.

Who got him? she asked.

"Them people got him, they snatched him up on suspicion of murder" he told her.

Boy, stop playin', put him on the phone, she said after a long pause.

"Listen, Nita, I wouldn't put no shit like that on that man, this some real shit, he left a voicemail, he 'posed to call back la—" he was saying but she cut him off.

Why didn't he call me?! she exclaimed feeling slightly offended. She was her woman, the same woman he shared a bed with every night. JC listened knowing that he had to cover for Richie Rich knowing how much he loved and cared for her, and he knew when a man had a woman, she felt obligated to know everything about that man, and he didn't wanna take that away from her, so he told her what he thought Richie would've wanted him to tell her.

"I'm assuming that he didn't wanna involve you in this shit more than he had to, you know him better than anybody, so you know how he is. Don't take it like he's cold shouldering you, that nigga love you, he just know I'm familiar with how shit goes, so he put that on me, you feel me?" he said.

I can understand that, she retorted. But when is he supposed to call you back? she asked.

"I was asleep when he called, but he said he gon' call back tonight, so for me to let you know what was up and to answer" JC added.

I'm finna leave and come back right now, so if he call, tell him to call me, my phone accept all of that shit, he the one that made me put it on there, she said frustrated.

"Aight, I will, but hurry up because you know that he only gon' be able to get one call, and you know them three ways be hanging up down there" he told her.

I'll be there a little after an hour, she said then hung up the phone. Nita was beyond fucked up in the head as she turned and looked at Tiera and Ciera with a distraught look on her face.

"What's wrong with you, girl? "Ciera asked after trying to ear hustle on her conversation as Tiera stood up, walked over, and sat on the couch next to Nita.

"We just gotta hurry up and get to Milwaukee, them people snatched Richie up, and he's gonna need me to be there" she said, and without uttering another word, she grabbed her purse and put on her shoes. "Y'all coming?" she asked while walking to the door as Tiera and Ciera quickly started grabbing their things as well. They definitely wasn't about to let her go by herself, when their friend was in distress, they were all in distress. "Hold up, I almost forgot my purse" Ciera said as she ran to her room and grabbed it, then she locked the door behind her after she left out of it.

******

"You know we're not going to be able to hold him if he doesn't implicate himself" Gomez said to Walsh who was sitting in a chair across from her drinking an energy drink.

"Yeah, I know" he said in a low tone, then he cleared his throat and exhaled in disappointment before he slammed the can on the table. "Let's go give it another round" he said getting up and staring at Gomez to see if she was in agreement.

"Why not? "she said. Although she was strictly by the book, she was in a new jurisdiction and didn't want to cause any rift raft towards her coworkers like she was being difficult, and they label her an outcast. Even though she knew by questioning Richie after he asked for a lawyer, they were subject to get the whole case thrown out. She was gonna ride with Walsh on this one because he had better knowledge of how they did things there. Getting up, she put her suit jacket on, and followed Walsh across the hall. Opening the door, they found Richie Rich laying back on the concrete bench with a roll of tissue under his head semi dosing off, he was tired and cold as hell.

"I see you're making yourself at home, that's what I like to see" Walsh smiled sarcastically while he stepped to the side to let Gomez in. "Get up" he continued.

"My lawyer here?" Richie sat up.

"Just come with us" Walsh spoke sternly. Richie Rich mugged him as he stood up and walked towards the exit with Walsh leading the way and Gomez right behind him. They purposely took him to another interrogation room that wasn't occupied with a video camera or a tape recorder. They did this knowing that they weren't supposed to be questioning him after he asked for a lawyer, so this was their way of trying to cover themselves just in case his lawyer got wind of this because they knew it would be Richie Rich's word against theirs. Walsh was confident his word stood firmly over any criminal. Walking in, Richie took a seat in the chair at the table feeling like something wasn't right, he just couldn't put his finger on it yet; then he watched as Gomez walked over and sat across from him and crossed her legs while staring Richie directly in the eyes. She had seen some of the toughest criminals in the country, and when she looked at Richie, she wouldn't say that he was one of them, but he had a certain confidence about himself, and it was enough to let her know that he wasn't going to tell them anything, but she had to give it her best try.

"So, Mr. Williams, are you willing to talk to us?" she asked.

"Didn't I tell y'all I'm not saying nothing til my lawyer gets here" he said pissed that they were on this bullshit.

"We gave you the chance to call your lawyer, but instead you called Mr. Cooper, so what do you want us to do about your decision?" she said before going into silence and just staring at him. A tactic they used called delayed action, it was with the intent of hoping that it would frustrate him, cause an overreaction, and he'd unconsciously start talking due to the silence, but Richie just looked pasted her; he stared at Walsh, giving him a mischievous grin.

"So, we gon' play these punk azz games, huh? You know like I do, y'all ain't got shit on me. Y'all think y'all slick gon' put me in this muthafuckin' room wit no camera or recorder because y'all know y'all don't 'posed to be questioning me after I asked for my lawyer, I know how this shit goes, just wait til my lawyer hears about this, I ain't new to this shit at all" Richie said, never breaking eye contact; and from the look on their faces, he knew he was right in his assessment of the situation.

Walsh got off the wall he was leaning on and walked over to Richie Rich. Leaning down towards his face so close that it caused Richie Rich to lean back, then Walsh put one hand on the table and his other hand on the arm of the chair. "You must have forgot we are the United States of America and your dumb dope dealing azz needs to start recognizing that. You know how many criminals come through here acting tough, but quickly realize that we are the law, and frankly, we can do what we want... Do you know what it takes to charge you with conspiracy? Well, let me educate you, more than one with the knowledge of illegal activity, add the guns, the murders that you committed, and there goes your RICO. By the time you see the streets again, a baby tree would have fully developed, got chopped down and turned into paper, so just think about that for a second... Matter of fact, think about Danita, James Cooper, and all them little idiots you got pushing those drugs for you... Oh, you didn't think I knew about them" Walsh chuckled after seeing the expression on Richie Rich's face.

"Now, I'm sure at least two of them, if not all of them will tell us whatever they know about your balling azz once we start throwing them numbers at them" he continued, then he gestured towards Gomez with a slight head nod that it was time to go, he was gonna give him a little more time to think about things after he revealed that he had some more information. He was hoping that Richie Rich would start to overthink things or become weary of what other information they had and start to panic. As Gomez got up; and followed Walsh to the door, Richie Rich asked.

"Can I call my people back now?" Richie asked.

Walsh looked back. We'll see, just sit tight for a minute" he said, then he closed the door and locked it.

"These muthafuckas" Richie Rich said while shaking his head.

Chapter Eighteen

* * * * *

It was approximately 12:24 pm when Nita rolled past the sign that said Welcome to Wisconsin. She couldn't wrap her mind around the suspicion of murder charge that JC said they were charging Richie Rich with because most of the time, she was with him while he was handling business. Now, she was far from a dumb woman, she knew what the life Richie was living entailed. She had uncles, cousins, and even her own mother who had their fair share of trouble with the law, so she understood the severity of the charges, and if he got convicted; she knew that could possibly be the end of him. Nita was vigilant attentive to where the sheriffs could be hiding as she sped through traffic doing 85 mph in her Lexus truck. Digging in her purse, she pulled her big Cartier sunglasses out, and put them on her face to stop the sun from beaming in her eyes.

As she replayed everything that took place before she left to go to Chicago, she came up with a good scenario after thinking about it. She remembered when they left Mayfair Mall, and JC asked her to stop at the gas station for some cigarettes, but she missed the turn because that white lady darted out in traffic and almost hit them, so when she avoided the collision, she missed the turn. Then him and Richie seen somebody they knew getting in or out of the car with a police officer. After that she was ear hustling the phone call JC had with the dude, but she couldn't fully grasp it, but then she remembered Richie say, we doing that shit tonight, so she knew that was possibly why he got snatched up, but what she couldn't figure out was why JC didn't get snatched to if he was with Richie? But Richie called him, so she didn't know what to think yet until he called and told her what was up, but she made a mental note to watch JC.

I knew he was up to something, I should've said something... she thought to herself, but Richie had been running the streets before she met him, that's how he got his money, so she didn't say much except for watch your back and be careful. She knew she had to let her man conduct his business the way he knew best, yeah, she knew about the streets, but she didn't know or understand what it was to be out there firsthand. As for the twins, Tiera was on the internet looking at the Frankie Matrullo website, a high fashion designer from Milwaukee, and Ciera was strolling through her timeline on Facebook. They had been around their friend long enough to know that she didn't wanna be bothered right now, she had a lot on her mind, so they kept the conversation to a minimum, they knew when she was ready to talk and vent, they'd be there for her to listen and give advice.

Nita just kept shaking her head at her thoughts of Richie Rich, she wondered was he alright? How did he get caught? When was his court date? What his bail was gonna be? Was he thinking about her? would the last time they made love be the day she left in the shower? She was already starting to feel a feeling of loss and a sense of abandonment, and it hadn't even been a whole 24-hours, but she loved the shit outta Richie Rich. In their short time together, he had displayed the signs of being a real man, and the way he treated her; separated him from any man or relationship that she has ever known, so she was definitely taking this hard.

After getting her mental mindset in order, she realized that she could very well lose him to Wisconsin's corrupt prison system, but she had plenty of fight left in her not to let that happen, and she knew he did as well, so she was gonna do whatever was necessary to get him out, or at least get him a life sentence, she made a mental note to Google top trial attorneys in Wisconsin when she got home. Reaching for her cellphone, she grabbed it, and called JC.

Hello, JC answered.

"Did he call yet?" she said before hitting her signal, looking over her shoulder, and switching lanes.

Nope, not yet......how far you is? JC asked.

"I'll be pulling up to my house in about ten or fifteen minutes" Nita said.

Aight, I gotta make a quick stop, but I should be sitting in your driveway when you pull up. I don't wanna sit on the street because y'all live way the fuck out, and them people out there nosy as fuck, they'll call the police on a nigga quick, JC replied.

"You already know that, that's why we moved out there" she said making him laugh. "I'll see you when I pull up, hopefully he still ain't called yet" she added.

Yeah, I know, in a minute, he said and ended the call.

******

"So, what's our next play?" Walsh asked Gomez for her opinion to see if they were on the same page. Although he was supposed to go by the book, at times in heavy pursuit, he could become a renegade which the attorney general was aware of. That's why they assigned Gomez to the case along with Walsh; she was there to keep him in line, and he knew that.

"Well...I'd say let him make his call, and hopefully someone slips up and says something that they weren't supposed to say, maybe the girlfriend, then we immediately put eyes and ears on them to obtain a stronger case to present to the grand jury... or... and this is a strong or...we let Richie Rich go..." she offered.

"Oh, hell no! I'm not letting this piece of shit out there" he interrupted her.

"You didn't let me finish" she said, feeling slightly offended.

"You're right, go ahead" he added.

"As I was saying, we could let him go, put eyes and ears on him, and let him hang himself even more. He's going to go back to dealing that's all he knows. Quincy did give him those kilos, so he has to sell them, and we'll be right there to catch him smack dead in the act, and we'll fry his azz for good and we'll get Mr. Cooper as well" Gomez said smiling. Walsh sat there for a minute deep in thought. "What you think about that?" she added.

"I actually like that idea" he smiled, then in one motion, he jumped to his feet, adjusted his pants, and straightened the shield that was clipped onto his belt. "Why not... but I think we should still keep him for another day, just to make him sweat" he added.

"Agreed, so you wanna give him his call?" Gomez asked.

"He can get it tomorrow" Walsh said with a self-satisfying look on his face.

"So, what do we do in the meantime?" Gomez said after glancing down at her watch.

"Let's go get a bite to eat" he said before opening the door and doing the ladies first gesture, then he followed her out, and closed the door behind him.

******

Richie Rich sat slumped down in the chair with his feet up on the table, fingers interlocked while twirling his thumbs. He knew they didn't have any evidence that he killed Quincy, but when they brought up Bubbles and the white girl Val, it had him thinking if he covered all of his tracks after all. Being stuck in that little azz room wasn't helping matters at all for his mental state either, he was feeling like they knew more than they were letting him know they knew. "Come on Richie, get yo shit together" he said out loud to himself.

Turning his thoughts to Nita, he wondered did she know he was locked up. Did JC get the message he left? Did he get knocked off, did he abandon ship and leave him hanging? He didn't know what the fuck was going on. Then he started to wonder what the fuck was taking Walsh's bitch azz so long to come back and give him his call. His mind was clearly becoming clouded. As he put his feet on the floor, he put his arms on the table and laid his head in them, zoned out, and unconsciously fell asleep.

Chapter Nineteen

* * * * *

J C circled the block a couple times to make sure there wasn't any suspicious looking cars out there before he pulled up and parked in front of the house Richie Rich shared with Nita in Wauwatosa. He said fuck it and didn't park in the driveway because if the Feds were on him, he wanted to be able to get up outta there if he had to. Turning Jeezy & Tee Grizzley's hit 'Cold Summer' down low, he sat back behind the tinted windows, fired up a blunt of Kush, and cracked the seal on his fif of Hennessy. Taking a few sips, he put the cap back on, and responded to a text from Miranda. Soon as he put his phone back in his pocket, he took a puff of his blunt and noticed Nita's truck pulling up in the driveway. After flashing his lights to let her know that was him, he finished smoking his blunt before he grabbed his book bag, bottle of Henny, got out of the car, hit the alarm, and entered the house.

"He still ain't calling?" Nita asked as soon as he entered the living room.

"Hell naw" JC responded and sat on the couch after putting his bag and bottle on the table. Pulling out his phone after he heard his text alert go off, it was Miranda. He quickly responded and put the phone back up, as soon as he did that, he instantly noticed Tiera and Ciera staring at him.

"What's hat-nen wit y'all?" he asked with a smile trying to see which one he felt liked him more, but they both seemed interested.

"Hey" they said in unison, they loved light skinned niggas, so they both were feeling him, and his style.

"What's y'all names?" he said.

"I'm Tiera" she said. "And I'm Ciera" her sister added.

"My name JC, nice to meet y'all...y'all smoke?" he offered.

"Yeah" Tiera said as JC went in his pocket pulled out a little over a half ounce of kush and four blunts and sat it on the table.

"Roll that up if you don't mind" he said, then picked up his bottle of Henny and hit that.

"Lemme hit some of that" Ciera said. Now, most niggas wouldn't let a bitch that they didn't know hit their bottle, but JC didn't mind because it was alcohol, so it was sterilizing as they sipped, so he passed her the bottle with no problem. He kept noticing the glances they were giving him, he knew they were feeling him, he wasn't thirsty at all, he was just gonna play it cool, and be him, and let that lead to what it was gon' lead to.

"I'll be right back" Nita said and disappeared into the back room.

While they did that, he opened up his book bag, and dumped the contents on the table. Out of his peripheral vision, he saw Tiera and Ciera staring as he picked up the money and started counting it out silently, he already knew that it was twenty-eight grand from the kilo he just sold, but he was just showing off. When Tiera finished rolling two of the blunts, she came and sat right next to him. "You got a lighter? "she asked.

"Yeah, here you go" he passed her the lighter, noticing how she made an extra effort to feel his hand when she took the lighter as Nita came back into the living room. Firing up the blunt, Tiera passed it to him, then fired up the next one, and passed it to Ciera before rolling the other two and putting them in rotation as well. They all smoked as Nita went in the kitchen and got some red plastic cups that they filled with Hennessy, and got lit. They were all in their high as hell and borderline drunk. JC finished playing with the money and went outside to put it in the safety of his car's trunk. Going back in the house, he told Nita that he had to use her bathroom. "You know where it is" she said making him laugh as he walked off.

"Girl, what's up with him?" Tiera asked Nita.

"For real though, that nigga fine, and he was in here counting them gees like it ain't nothing" Ciera said.

"That's Richie's guy, that's all I know" Nita said.

"He finna be my guy now, after I give him some of this pussy" Tiera smile feeling the effects of the liquor and weed.

"Uh-uh, I'm finna fuck him, and Imma introduce him to the throat goat" Ciera smiled as Nita and Tiera laughed.

"Bitch, you is stupid" Nita commented while still laughing.

"You always tryna step on my toes, it's already bad enough you look like me" Tiera spoke.

"So, we always in competition, may the best pussy and head win" Ciera smiled.

"Wait a minute, both of y'all finna fuck him?" Nita asked shaking her head.

"Hell yeah" the twins said in unison.

"This won't be the first time we done it" Tiera said. "Matter of fact, I'm going first" she added while getting up and heading towards the back.

"Naw, bitch, we gon' do it together" Ciera said.

"Come on then" Tiera said.

"Y'all finna have a threesome with that nigga?" Nita said with her face frowned up.

"Yeah, well... kinda, we don't gotta touch on each other to bust this nigga down" Ciera said.

"Listen, Imma get him in the room first, then you come in" Tiera said.

"Okay go ahead" Ciera replied.

"Y'all bitches a mess" Nita commented and shook her head.

******

Waking up from the uncomfortable nap in his arms, Richie sat up cold as hell like they turned the air-conditioning on to torture him. Putting his arms inside the jail t-shirt that they gave him in effort to warm himself up, then he began to move his neck around to work out the crook that he felt coming on. "This shit crazy" he said in frustration while getting up on his feet, then he walked over to the steel toilet to take a piss. After handling his business, he washed his hands, then he went to the door, and started pounding on it to get somebody's attention, it was too fuckin' cold in there, seeing nobody was coming, he turned around and used the bottom of his shoe and kicked the door three times.

"Punk azz muthafuckas" he added, then he went to sit back down. Staring straight into the wall with a blank look on his face, he started to think about Nita and his money. This shit was really starting to fuck with him because he was unsure if the Feds ran in his shit and tore it up, or what. He knew Nita should be back already, and the words Walsh said came back into his mind. *That girl you got is gonna run off with JC and have his baby while spending your money...* He wondered if that could be true.

"Man, I'm trippin', I'm in this bitch goin' crazy already" he said out loud to himself. He didn't know what time it was because it wasn't a clock in there, but it felt like he had been in there for weeks, he needed to get his shit together, he had to maintain his focus if he was gonna get outta this jam.

******

JC finished taking a piss, wiped the seat off, flushed the toilet, and washed his hands. After shaking his hands dry, he looked himself over in the mirror, and liked what he seen. Opening the bathroom door, he turned the light out, and walked down the hallway leading back to the living room. As he walked past the guest room, he seen Tiera stick her head out, he only knew it was her because she wore a different hairstyle than Ciera.

"JC" she said.

"What's hat-nen?" he inquired.

"I need you to come help me with something" she smiled mischievously, and without a second thought, JC walked into the room to see what she needed his help with.

"What you need me to do?" he asked looking around curiously as he was wondering what she was on. Tiera smiled as she walked over to him seductively and tongue kissed him throwing JC completely off, but he didn't contest it, he just put his hands around her back, squeezed and rubbed his hands all over her plump ass. Then the door opened up and Ciera walked in, causing them to break their embrace, but JC was even more surprised by what she said.

"Bitch, we supposed to do it together" she said as she walked over to where they stood.

"You was taking too long" Tiera said stepping back and pulling her shirt over her head exposing double D-cup breasts, as she was taking her pants off, Ciera was tongue kissing JC. He couldn't believe what was happening, he was a player type nigga, but he can honestly say he hadn't seen this coming. He thought he would be able to fuck one of them before the night was over, but to have them both, being they were not only sisters, but twin sisters. His player card was about to skyrocket a lot of notches if he could pull this off.

Dropping down to her knees, Ciera unbuckled his belt, unfastened his pants, and put her hand in his boxers pulling out his fully erect dick. Ciera mastered the head game, and she was proud about it, she loved having the power to make a nigga weak in the knees, to have them begging her to stop or to keep going, so if she liked a nigga, she was never shy to suck that dick, and have him blowing up her phone, she hadn't failed yet. She moaned, loving the size of what he was working with; looking him in his eyes, she stuck her pierced tongue out and circled the head of his dick with it before tracing the thick veined underside with her tongue. JC pulled his shirt over his head and threw it on the chair just as Tiera walked up removing her bra. JC immediately grabbed her titties and latched on to one of her nipples, sucking it hard. Just as he did that, Ciera slid his dick halfway in her mouth. JC immediately stopped sucking the titties and looked down at her. "Shhhiiiit" he said realizing she was different with the head, and he meant that in every good way possible.

Ciera was in her element when performing oral sex as she backed off of the dick before sliding him all the way down her throat. JC took a step back; she was savagery with the head game. "Uh uh, where you going?" Ciera smiled, she hadn't met a nigga yet that could last from what she did best.

Pushing him back on the bed, she pulled his pants and boxers all the way off after he stepped outta his shoes, then she opened his legs up, got in between them, and went right back to sucking his dick as Tiera kneeled next to her. "Let me get some of that" she said as Ciera passed his dick to her like they were passing a blunt. Tiera grabbed him, then she put him in her mouth and gave him some slow sensual head, as Ciera got up and removed all of her clothing. "Awww, fuck..." JC moaned out, they weren't fuckin' around with him.

"Nigga, stop whining, I got something for you" Ciera said taking off her panties, then she stepped in the bed, put her leg over his head, and lowered her pussy down onto his face. JC stuck his tongue out and let her sit on it. On the inside, JC was smiling hard as hell, he had a mouth on his dick, a pussy on his face, and this was his first threesome ever, shit couldn't get any better than what he was doing right now. After a few minutes, the girls switched then got right back to getting it in. But that was short-lived because JC had to stop Ciera before she made him bust, she was doing too much.

Tiera got in the bed and directly into the doggy style position, JC got right behind her with Ciera next to him. Ciera grabbed his dick, stroking him as she kissed him. JC smacked Tiera's ass, then Ciera spread her sister's ass cheeks and told JC to hold them open, then she spanked Tiera's pussy with JC's dick before sliding it in. JC began his stroke game as he sucked Ciera's titties while she held Tiera's ass open for him to get deeper. Tiera got to throwing that ass back on him and he was meeting her, thrust for thrust. JC loved when he had a woman who knew how to throw that ass back as she did. Ciera leaned over and hawked up some spit then she spat directly into Tiera's winking ass hole. Leaning over, she told

JC to put his finger in there, and he obliged; she knew exactly what her sister liked. JC continued to hit her from the back and work his finger in her ass hole. "Ooooh, fuck me" Tiera moaned before putting her head into the pillow and raising her ass up even higher. JC was fuckin' the shit outta her, but he knew he had to slow it down because he wanted to fuck Ciera too. Pulling his dick outta Tiera, he looked at Ciera. "Suck this dick clean" he told her.

"That aggressive shit turns me the fuck on" Ciera said while grabbing his dick and going right down to do what he requested, sucking all of her sister's pussy juices off of it, much to JC's delight. Pulling himself outta her mouth because he could tell that she was tryna make him bust, he had other plans. Laying down, Ciera mounted him, grabbed his dick, and slid down on it as Tiera got on his face and rode it. Although the sisters were riding different parts of him, they both had the same objective, and that was to cum. JC gripped Ciera's ass as she rode him like she was Pinky, Roxy Reynolds, or somebody, until she felt herself being unable to control what was coming. "I'm cummin" she said in a high pitch tone and began to release her juices down his pipe.

Hearing her sister reach her peak mixed with the tongue to clit action that she was getting from JC as she rode his face, it was inevitable that she came too. "I'm cummin" she said lowly as her body went through a short convulsion before her cum ran outta her and into JC's mouth. "Ummm" he said not expecting her to have that much coming down, he was so caught up in the session that he let her cum in his mouth, knowing he was bogus. Tiera got off of his face and he looked at her. "You tried to drown me with that shit, huh?" he said as they both laughed while Ciera got off of his dick. "I'm sorry baby, I can cum a lot" Tiera said.

"I see" he said wiping his mouth as they continued to laugh.

"Well, he hasn't cum yet, which I am surprised about, he gotta be the first to last through an entire session, you might get to fuck us again just off of that, dick stayed hard too" Ciera said impressed and JC was all smiles after hearing that. "Let's both do something special for him to get him off" she continued as she grabbed his hand and helped him get outta bed and onto his feet. Ciera and Tiera then both kneeled before him, and Tiera grabbed his dick and began to suck it slowly with plenty of eye contact. Then she passed it to Ciera, and she sucked him at an ultimate slow level, causing his toes to curl, then she passed it back to Tiera who grabbed it and slapped it on her tongue three times before she put both hands around his shaft and twisted it as she suck him. JC was losing his damn mind; them hoes were literally tryna suck the life outta him. Then she stopped and passed it back to Ciera. "Finish him off, sis" she said knowing that was her sister's specialty.

"You been tryna outlast me all day, well that shit is over with, I'm finna get it up outta you in a minute or less" Ciera said then she put him in her mouth, and the first bob of her head was like she went on super vacuum mode, she was going in. JC tried to step back, but she pulled him right back to her and continued her oral stimulation on him while him and Tiera watched.

"I'm finna cum...!" JC yelled out.

"Give it to us" Tiera said as she put her face next to Ciera's as he pulled his dick outta her mouth and jagged it off.

"Oh shit" he said as he busted his nut all over both of their faces and mouths. They moaned in unison as he smeared it on their faces using his dick. Then he stuck it back into Ciera's mouth, her head was serious, he could get used to something like that on the regular. Seeing them both kneeling in front of him with his nut still on their faces and mouths, he started to feel like the man, and he wanted to see how far he could push it.

"Yeah, suck that dick" he told Ciera and she stayed focused on that. "Now let your sister suck it" he added and she passed it to Tiera making him smile; after a minute or so, he took it out of her mouth. "Now kiss her" he continued as they kissed between the cum on their lips. JC loved that shit, and it was evident because his dick had yet to go flaccid.

"I gotta clean this shit off of my face" Tiera said while getting up.

"Me too, this nigga even got some in my hair, I hope I can get an hair appointment on you, JC?" Ciera asked seriously.

"I got both of y'all, no problem" he said in hopes that he could have both of them as he slid his boxers back on.

"I know you do, baby" Ciera said as she grabbed her things and kissed his lips as she left out of the door.

"Thank you, baby, I hope you enjoyed yourself" Tiera said as she kissed him on the lips too, then she grabbed her shoes and left out of the room.

JC finished getting dressed, then he sat on the bed feeling brand new after he just took down a set of twins, he didn't know another nigga who had accomplished that feat, he couldn't wait to tell Richie Rich, he wasn't gon' believe it.

******

After cleaning herself up, Tiera came out of the bathroom and walked into the living room with a smirk on her face as she sat on the sofa.

"Girl…" Ciera began. "That nigga was in there performing on both of y'all asses and kept it up the whole time" Nita said searching for confirmation that what she heard was indeed true.

"Hell yeah, he definitely holdin', he know how to fuck and lick a bitch the right way" Tiera smiled.

"I told you, I'm too much for a nigga by myself, this nigga fucked both of us, we suck his dick and he was still turnt, and ready to go, it had to be the alcohol. I could definitely fuck with a nigga like that for real, and he getting to the paper too. I might have to be that nigga's wifey" Ciera smiled.

"We, bitch, we sharing him until he make a choice" Tiera said.

"We both know he's gonna choose me, you seen that nigga runnin' from that head" she said as Nita was moving her head from side to side trying to listen to what each of them were saying.

"My head ain't shabby at all, and my pussy better, you see what it was from the back" Tiera added.

"Bitch, please, that pussy as wide as your shirt collar" Ciera laughed.

"Yeah, okay" Tiera retorted.

"Wait, wait, wait, you hoes in here really trippin'. Both of y'all fucked him and equally liked it, obviously he did, too. Y'all arguing for no reason, he gon' cash y'all hoping he can get that again. How y'all gon' let a dick come between y'all...y'all trippin'. It's a win-win. Even if he starts fuckin' wit one of y'all, you can always bring the other in and he gon' cash y'all to feel that, I guarantee you that" Nita spoke logically.

"Yeah, you're right" Tiera said after thinking about it.

"Sorry, sis" Ciera said apologetically.

"I'm sorry, too" Tiera said.

"That's more like it" Nita said, and before she could speak any further on the situation, JC came from the back.

"Y'all hungry? Somebody call and order some pizzas, it's on me, order whatever y'all want and tell them to bring a few two-liter sodas too, I'm finna go get the box of blunts out of the car, I'll be right back" he said before dropping a hundred and twenty dollars on the table. Cutting his eyes at Ciera and Tiera he then winked at them on his way out.

"I think y'all bitches in love" Nita said as they all laughed.

******

The next morning, Richie Rich sat in the chair deep in thought, when he heard the door finally open up. Turning his head towards the door, he saw Gomez and Walsh walk through the door, but the way they were positioned, it looked to be like a clear path out, but he didn't understand it, he didn't wanna give them any reason to get on any police brutality shit. He knew how the police ached to get at an unarmed black man and claim they were defending themselves or he was trying to escape, or grab their gun, the typical shit. Unsure of what they were on as they just stood there looking at him, he spoke up. "What's hat-nen? Y'all finna give me my call now?" Richie asked.

"Make it on your own time, you're free to go" Gomez said with a stern look on her face.

Hearing this, Richie's eyes immediately darted towards Walsh for confirmation, thinking that Gomez was bullshitting. The disappointed and uncertain expression on his face let Richie know she was telling the truth. Getting to his feet, he walked towards the door and stopped right in front of Walsh with a smirk on his face.

"Oh, it's far from over!" Walsh said while staring him down.

"Is that a threat?" Richie smiled." Wait til my lawyer hears about all of this" he added.

"Okay, Mr. Williams, get going before I change my mind" Gomez snapped.

"Now, how I'm gon' get home?" Richie asked.

Walsh looked at him, then towards Gomez who shrugged her shoulders, then he smirked and said. "You know what?... You going out to that place in Wauwatosa?"

Richie frowned his face up and looked at him like he was crazy. "Yeah" he added.

"I told you I know everything" Walsh smiled. "So, is that where you're going?" he continued.

"Yeah" he answered.

"Well, you might as well let us drop you off, then you ain't gotta have that pretty girl come all the way down here, and who knows...they don't know that you're getting out, you might catch JC over there" Walsh shot a shot at him and chuckled.

"Let's go, then" Richie Rich said against his better judgement, he wanted to see what was going on.

"You coming?" Walsh asked Gomez as she looked down at her watch, then started to follow them down the hallway and out to the car. She knew Walsh was up to something, but she didn't know what yet.

Chapter Twenty

* * * * *

The sun was starting to set as Nita got out of bed to stretch her legs. Sliding into a pair of leggings, she went into the bathroom that was connected to the master bedroom and handled her hygiene, then she came back into her room, unlocked the door, and walked into the living room. She saw Tiera on the couch in the fetal position under a sheet. JC was asleep on a pallet on the floor, with his head back and mouth slightly open. Turning, she saw Ciera come out of the kitchen with some pizza and a bottled water. When Ciera saw her, she waved her towards the kitchen, and then walked back in there herself. "It's about time yo azz got up" Ciera smiled.

"Why?... What did you do now, bitch? I see that smirk on your face" Nita questioned.

"When you went to bed last night, I kept filling Tiera's cup with that Henny knowing that bitch gets sleepy as hell when she gets drunk... and as soon as she went to sleep, I took JC's fine azz in that room, and we fucked and sucked each other all night long literally, we just came out the room about an hour ago" Ciera smiled.

"Bitch, you petty as hell for that, I thought y'all was gon' share him?" Nita replied.

"And we will, I just needed to fuck him by myself, I sucked that nigga's dick for an hour straight, swallowed all that shit, he ain't gon' ever forget me, trust that" Ciera laughed.

"I bet he ain't, wit yo nasty azz" Nita smiled.

"That's what he said, too" she said as they laughed.

"Let's go outside, sit on the porch, and talk" Nita suggested.

"Come on" Ciera said as she picked her plate of pizza up and followed Nita to the front door. As they got to the door, Ciera tripped over a pair of shoes and almost fell; the noise she made woke Tiera up, but she just laid there, and didn't move.

"Look at yo maladroit azz" Nita laughed as she opened the front door.

"What the fuck that mean?" she retorted.

"Clumsy bitch, damn. Won't you try reading a book instead of sucking all them dicks" Nita said making her laugh as they headed out to the porch and closed the door behind them.

Soon as Tiera heard the door close, she hopped up, looked toward JC who was still asleep on the floor, she smiled, and quickly made her way to the bathroom. After using it, she washed her hands, then she put some toothpaste on her finger and ran it across her teeth and on her tongue, after rinsing her mouth out, she looked in the mirror and smiled at what she seen. Then she hurriedly made her way back into the living room and woke JC up. "JC... JC" she said while shaking him awake.

"What's up?" he said, opening his eyes.

"Come on, while they outside" she smiled and he knew exactly what she meant, but he was tired. Tiera had no idea that he was up fucking her sister all night. However, he was not ever the one to back down from a challenge, so he got up knowing he'd muster up the strength once she got naked. Grabbing his hand, she led him into the guest room, closed the door and locked it, then she peeled her leggings from her body and got in the doggy style position on the edge of the bed. Seeing all that ass, JC shook his head, took his shirt off, and undid his pants before pulling out his fully erect dick, and getting right behind her. Smacking her ass, a couple of times to see it wiggle, he spat on his index and middle finger and put them inside of her pussy to moisten her, then he slid his already swollen member inside of her.

"Ooooh baby, shiiiit" she moaned as he slow stroked her. JC smiled. These twins were freaks, and as long as they were willing to, he was going to provide it.

******

"Girl, Ion't know what the fuck goin' on, they snatched my man up, and he ain't even called yet to let me know what's up, what he need me to do or nothing" Nita exhaled and shook her head.

"You gotta be strong, baby" Ciera said while rubbing her back.

"I'm trying to" she sniffled with her head down.

"Who the fuck is that?" Ciera asked as she watched the grey Crown Victoria pull up in front of the house and park on the opposite side of the street. Raising her head up, Nita looked. "That's the police bitch, I hope they ain't coming over here" she added. Nita and Ciera kept staring at the white man driving, and what looked to be a female in the passenger seat.

"Girl, it's somebody in the backseat" Ciera said as the white man got out of the car and opened up the back door and Richie Rich stepped out.

"Richie, my baby!" Nita exclaimed as she got up from her seat and ran to the curb as he came across the street and grabbed her up in his arms, squeezed her ass and hugged him.

******

"Fuck!" JC said after he came deep inside of Tiera when he heard some yelling. "You heard that?" he continued as Tiera looked back at him still in the doggy style position.

"Yeah, it sounded like somebody called Richie's name" she said.

"Huh? Let's go see" he said before sliding out of her, wiping his dick off on the towel, then pulled his pants up, and put his shirt back on as Tiera put her leggings and sandals back on while trying to run her hands through her hair to fix it. After they were both straight, they left out of the room, and just as they made it to the living room, Ciera was coming through the front door looking suspicious because she knew what they had been up to, but it was a bigger task at hand.

"I need to talk to you now!" Ciera told her sister and headed towards the back. Knowing her sister, Tiera knew it was something serious, so she followed her towards the back and into the bathroom. JC stood there looking dumbfounded, he was under the impression that Ciera was mad because he fucked her all night, and he knew she that she knew he just fucked Tiera too.

"Damn, I fucked that up already" he said out loud to himself and shook his head as he went to go sit on the couch.

******

"I'll be seeing you soon" Walsh said sarcastically before he rolled his window up and pulled off.

"I wouldn't count on no shit like that" Richie shot back.

"If I were you, Danita, I'd get as far as possible away from that man" Walsh looked at Nita.

"Man, get the fuck on" Richie snarled while staring him down as they drove down the block. "Fat bitch azz" he added.

"Baby, what they on with you?" Nita asked, worried.

"Just tryna fuck wit me, they ain't got shit on me" he said.

"Why you ain't call?" she asked him.

"I did one time, that nigga JC ain't answer, then them bitches gotta playing games and wouldn't let me call no more, then they come let me out today, they think they slick, they watching me and waiting on me to bust a move, so they can get on that, but fuck that" he said looking her in the eyes.

"The nigga JC in there now, we been here all-night waiting on your call" Nita said.

"I can see that" he said letting her go from his embrace when he saw JC's car parked out front. Nita noticed the shift in his demeanor, and she could tell that he was on some jealous shit, so she wanted to shut that down before it ever formed into a damaging thought.

"Richie don't play wit me...he in there fuckin' the twins, is that what you think of me?" she asked slightly offended. Seeing that he had struck a nerve when he in fact knew better, he did a little damage control.

"Naw, baby,I was just fuckin' with you, I know better...come here" he said and pulled her back into his arms and kissed her.

"Cause I was finna say..." she said letting her anger subside.

"You wasn't finna say shit, bring yo azz on in this house" he spoke sternly trying to throw her off from what he was initially thinking.

"You just take your azz right to the bedroom" she said.

"You already know that" he replied.

JC looked towards the door when he heard a male's voice coming into the house talking. Seeing it was Richie Rich, he jumped up, and met him at the living room entrance. "My nigga, what the fuck happened? We been waiting on you to call, I got—" JC said.

"Man, these people on some bullshit, lemme go handle something, then I'm finna come right back and slide on you" Richie said.

******

"Where y'all at?" Nita said as she walked down the hall.

"We in here" Ciera said as she opened the bathroom door and let Nita in. When she stepped in Tiera was in the mirror tryna fluff her hair out, then she stopped when Nita came in.

"What are y'all doing all cooped up in my bathroom? My man don't like y'all running through our shit like this" she said.

"Yo man, huh?" Ciera asked sarcastically.

"That's what I said, and what is that sarcastic azz shit 'posed to mean?" she shot back.

"How that shit looked today, then?" Ciera asked.

"What are you talking about?" Nita asked inquisitively while trying to recollect what she was speaking of.

"Bitch, why that nigga get dropped off by the police?" Tiera spoke up after seeing Nita was taking too long.

"So, what y'all tryna say?" she asked.

Ciera grabbed her arms like she was bracing her for a notification of death, taking a deep breath because although she needed to say what was about to be said, this was her friend, and she didn't want to hurt her, but she had to say something. Standing there in silence for what seemed like eternity, Nita spoke up. "What?!"

"I'm just gon' say it... I think Richie Rich snitchin'" Ciera came out with it.

"You bitches sound stupid right now...why would you say some stupid shit like that?" Nita spoke and shook her arms loose from Ciera's grip.

"Why would we say something like that? Bitch, use your head, he just got dropped off by the fuckin' police... Front door service, where the fuck they do that at? If he was in the city, his azz would've got killed as soon as he got out of that car. This nigga a drug dealer, a known drug dealer at that, the shit is not rocket science" Ciera scolded her.

"That shit is quite suspect" Tiera added her two cents.

"Okay, and... what y'all want me to do?" Nita asked.

"And?...really bitch, I know you just didn't say no stupid shit like that, that's why my brother gone right now, for a nigga not being able to hold their own weight, so you can take his side if you want to, but I refuse to lose you to the same circumstances, I've had your best interest at hand way before dude ever came into your life, obviously he don't, or he wouldn't have put you in this position" Ciera said staring at her friend since middle school. After a long pause that seemed like forever, Nita spoke knowing what she said was accurate.

"I wasn't taking his side in the sense of going against y'all. I just got feelings for him, but not enough to go to jail for him. So, when I said what y'all want me to do, I meant it as about dealing with him" she said, trying to reassure them of her disapproval for snitching no matter her connection to the accused, but she truly loved Richie Rich, so she was in a serious dilemma.

"That's more like it" Ciera smiled.

******

"You done, bro?" JC asked.

"Hell yeah, how the fuck Imma enjoy the fruits of my labor from a prison cell? With commissary? Hell naw, I'm telling you this shit ain't gon' end well if a muthafucka don't step away now" Richie said.

JC couldn't believe Richie Rich was sitting in front of him waving the white flag like this. Before he got knocked, he was just schooling JC on how to conduct shit in the streets, now he was wondering where all that boss shit he used to be about was right now. JC understood that them people may be on them, but how bad could it really be if they let Richie Rich out after they locked him up? Shit just wasn't adding up. "So, if you done, what we gon' do about the work we got now?" JC asked.

"You still finna fuck around?" Richie snapped.

"Hell yeah, I'm out here" JC fired back.

Richie Rich looked at him a little surprised because he thought JC had more sense than that, but after that response, he started to question that, especially with knowing what he just told him. But that was his life, and he was gon' live it the way he wanted to. Richie appreciated his loyalty, he was a good solid nigga, so he was gon' try to make this as easy as possible for both of them.

"I'll tell you what, Imma keep the two hundred and fifty Gs that I was supposed to drop off to Quincy, and you keep the ten bricks, which is more than my portion depending on how you bust it down. I know I'm getting the fuck outta here, so I need the cash... You think that's fair?" Richie asked.

"I was looking forward to us getting out here together bro, no lie. When I crawl through the mud wit a nigga, it's only right that I ball wit that nigga, you feel me?" JC said as Richie acknowledged his words with a head nod. "But yeah bro, if you're really done, then I'll take the ten and finesse those as best as I can" he added.

"Aight, let me go take care of what I gotta do, then we'll go to my stash house and grab that shit for you, I gotta get my Benz from over the other house anyways" Richie said while standing to his feet."

Aight, bet" JC said sitting back smiling as his mind started to form into just how he was about to get out here and distribute the work, and enjoy his newfound stardom that was sure to come with his new wealth. As Richie Rich headed up the stairs, he started to yell for his woman. "Nita!"

******

On the ride back to the downtown police station, Walsh didn't say a word to Gomez, which didn't bother her one bit. As Walsh drove, he started to regret the choice to let Richie Rich out after they had him locked up already. He was in fear that Richie would ghost on him, or caused harm to somebody else while out there, and that pissed him off. He was feeling like all of his efforts were going in vain. Glancing over in Gomez's direction, he frowned his face up at her, but she didn't see him because she was looking out of the window. Walsh's frustration had reached a boiling point, and that was evident by what he said after taking a long hard deep breath. "You know what? You're a bitch" he told her.

"Excuse me?" Gomez said angrily while looking towards him.

"I don't like you or your approach to things. You challenged me and convinced me to let a dangerous man back out here on these streets... his azz should still be locked up, and if kills someone else, that's on you" Walsh said harshly.

"And you call me a bitch, but you're the one acting like it's your time of the month. I don't give a damn if you don't like me, you will respect me" Gomez unleashed some of her Spanish sassiness on him. "As soon as we get back, I'm faxing

195

the attorney general and tell him to get me as far away from your stupid azz as possible" she added.

"Yeah, do that!" he said after a pause.

"The way you're operating out here, you're gonna get yourself killed, and I don't want to have anything to do with it" Gomez said rolling her neck as he turned to meet her piercing stare. "What?" she added.

"Just make sure you put that fax in" Walsh retorted.

******

"Tell me what to..." Nita started but stopped when she heard Richie Rich calling her. "He callin' me, we gotta go" she told Ciera and Tiera frantically.

"Kill that nigga, Nita, that police azz nigga gotta go" Ciera said in a low aggressive tone while she stared at her without blinking.

Nita eyes got extremely wide, she was expecting them to tell her to leave him, but to kill him, she wasn't so sure if she could do it. "Who gon' kill him?" Nita asked.

"You got to, you the only one that can get that close to him" Ciera spoke.

"Listen, I don't care, but I'm not doin' it" Nita said.

"You gotta do it" Tiera chimed in.

"Whatever, we'll talk about this later, let's get outta this bathroom before he becomes suspicious, because one thing that he isn't is stupid" Nita said while turning around and reaching for the doorknob.

"We'll definitely will talk about it later, but we can't wait too long, this game got a shot clock, and if we don't move accordingly, we could lose our possession to somebody who doesn't have our best interest at hand... and I'm not gonna let you lose to that nigga or any other nigga ever, you hear me?" Ciera spoke.

Nita nodded her head in acknowledgement, then she turned the door handle, and opened the door. Her heart immediately sank when she seen Richie Rich standing right there because she didn't know if he heard them talking or what, so she was literally stuck until he spoke.

"Damn, what the fuck y'all doin' in there?" he said with his face frowned up. As soon as Nita was about say something, Ciera did because she felt like Richie Rich shouldn't even be opening his mouth questioning what they were doing when he had a big question mark over his head, and she let that be known.

"You should be telling Nita what you was doin' getting dropped off by them people" Ciera said bluntly just as JC walked up and heard what was going on loud and clear.

"Bitch, what? You supa thot azz hoe, if you ever put some shit like that on my name, Imma break yo muthafuckin' eye socket, you weak azz bitch" Richie went livid, then tried to spit on her.

JC didn't know how Richie Rich got there, it all made sense to him why when Ciera came into the house and told Tiera that she needed to talk to her and they disappeared into the back. Now he knew exactly what the conversation was about. His mind started racing, they just bodied a muthafucka for snitchin', so how could he turn around and do it? He couldn't have...then he began to wonder is that why Richie was calling it quits and giving him all the dope, so he could get him set up? But his biggest question to himself was... how the fuck did Richie get outta jail so soon on a murder charge before his 72-hour questioning hold? Shit wasn't adding up to JC at all, he refused to be played at any point, but he stayed silent as he stood there listening to them go back and forth.

"Did you just try to spit on me? Why you gettin' so defensive, you got somethin' to hide?" Ciera smirked.

"Bitch, my name great in the streets and I seen some shit Jehovah ain't even witnessed, and been through more than that, so you need to watch yo fuckin' mouth when you don't know what the fuck you talkin' bout" Richie fired back and then he heard Tiera smack her teeth, which pissed him off even more. "You know what? Both of you broke azz punk azz hoes can get the fuck out my shit and take y'all dusty azzes back to Chicago" he added while pointing towards the door.

"Richie" Nita said, but he wasn't tryna hear none of that shit.

"Come on, let's go, get the fuck up out my shit, before I beat both you bitches azz for that blatant disrespect" he said while escorting them to the door and opening it up. "Let's go, right now" he continued.

In the process of the twins grabbing their things, Tiera looked over to Nita and asked her. "Are you coming?"

Nita closed her eyes and shook her head before Richie turned to see it. After grabbing their shit, they both kissed JC on the lips, and headed out the other door. Ciera turned around and said "Don't forget" then left.

"You hoes already forgot" Richie said while closing the door on the back of her heels as she left out of the house. "Fuck y'all!" he yelled before closing the door. Walking back into the living room, Richie told Nita "I don't wanna see them bitches back in my shit no more, you hear me?" he demanded.

"Yeah, I hear you" she responded.

"Come on, JC, let's get in traffic and go handle this business. We still goin' along with the plan from, earlier right?" Richie asked.

"Absolutely" JC said as he got off other couch and started walking towards the door, but stopped when he saw Richie walk up to Nita and whisper something in her ear.

While Richie talked, JC noticed Nita's eyes glance in his direction which cause him to be filled with paranoia as to what they were speaking about. He just knew that it was something about him since Nita couldn't control her eyes. Stepping back, Richie kissed her lips and grabbed his keys. "I'll be back, make sure that you have everything ready" he told her.

JC went numb for a minute, as he just tried to register what Richie Rich just told Nita, and not in the way Richie said it, he was processing it as the way he interpreted it. "You ready?" JC said still trying to figure out what was going on.

"Let's ride" Richie said and grabbed his .45 extendo from inside of the TV stand and put it inside of his waistband.

That was there the whole time... JC thought to himself. Then they walked outside, where Richie opened the garage and backed the Cutlass out while rolling the window down. "You want me to follow you?" JC asked.

"Naw, you can leave yo shit here, the Benz got a stash so we'll make it back and you can go straight up North Avenue and hop on the freeway to get to yo crib" Richie spoke as JC nodded... as he was getting into the passenger side, he saw Nita looking out of the window looking suspicious to him as Richie backed the rest of the way outta the garage, then smashed off.

Chapter Twenty-One

* * * * *

N ita had just gotten out of the shower and, after handling her hygiene, she lotioned her body down. Then she put on a pair of blue booty shorts, a white tank top with no bra, and tied her hair in a bun atop of her head. Then she grabbed her cellphone, the automatic money counter, and went downstairs to the living room. Grabbing the garbage bag, she dumped the contents on the table, grabbed a stack of bills, made sure they were even, then she stuffed the large stack into the money counter, and pressed the button. As that was happening, she went into the kitchen's drawer and got the bag of rubber bands, a pen, and a small note pad before making her way back into the living room just as the money counter finished. Nita wrote down the numbers on the pad, then rubber banded it, and put the stack off to the side before doing the next stack the exact same way. About thirty minutes into her counting, her cellphone rang. Placing the money back on the table, she answered. "Hello" she said.

He gone yet? Ciera asked.

"Yeah, where y'all at?" she added.

At that burger place by yo house. Shit, you know we rode with you back here, so we ain't got no ride back home, Ciera said.

"Well, come on back, he prolly be gon' for a minute, he gon' call me anyway, so Imma either take y'all back or have somebody drop y'all off" Nita told her.

Okay, we'll be there in about ten minutes, we eating right now, but we'll see you in a minute, Ciera laughed.

"I'll see y'all when y'all get here" Nita said then hung up the phone and put it back on the table.

After about ten more minutes of running the money through the counter, she threw everything back into the garbage bag and put it in her hallway closet by the front door. She didn't want the twins to see it. Not that she didn't trust them, she just felt like money always complicated things and situations. Soon as she closed the closet door, she peeked out of her front door and seen the twins walking towards the house, so she opened the door and went back to sit on the couch, picking up her phone, she checked the GPS on Richie's find-my-phone app, so that she could find out his location. Seeing he wasn't close to the house, she placed the phone back down.

"Nita, I'm tryna figure out what we about to do about this, because if you just gon' keep fuckin' wit dude, we finna go back to the Chi,I ain't even tryna be around him like that no more" Ciera said, pissed off.

"Who you tellin', I'm sick and tired of these hoe azz niggas up here already" Tiera commented as she and Ciera walked into the living room.

Nita sat there knowing what they wanted to hear from her as they kept babbling on and on until she got the point. "Sit down" Nita told them. The moment she was about to open her mouth, her cellphone rang. Grabbing the phone, she looked at the screen and saw it was Richie Rich, then she put up one finger before she answered it.

"What's up, bae?" she asked.

Did you handle what we talked about yet? he asked her.

"I'm getting on top of that as we speak" Nita replied.

So, what it's lookin' like? he asked.

"Bae, let me finish first, and I'mma hit you back and let you know if you not already back yet" she said.

Aight, just make sure everything ready to go, he said as he caught JC give him a weird look out of his peripheral vision as he hung the phone up.

"Who was that, snitchie Richie bitchie azz?" Ciera asked, laughing.

"You already know" she responded.

"I don't know how you could even still fuck wit dude after seeing him get out that police car" Ciera said and rolled her eyes. "What he want anyways?" she added.

203

"He wants me to count his money up because we about to get outta here." Nita said.

"What?!" Tiera exclaimed.

"Oh, hell naw!" Ciera chimed in.

"I'm not going, calm the fuck down! I just told him I was on top of it, but check this out" Nita said, but the tone in her voice caused both sisters to move over closer to where she was sitting, so that they could give her their undivided attention. "Listen, why can't we just peel him for the money, I'm really not with this killing him thing" she continued.

"Bitch, you had us move over here to say that shit" Ciera huffed, disappointed.

"Yeah, because it's still gon' hurt him and he not gon' come looking for it, so we might as well just take it, and if he really snitchin', the streets gon' take care of that" she said.

"You sound stupid as hell, you take a couple hundred Gs from a nigga, he definitely coming to look for you. The nigga was just locked up for suspicion of murder, so he got that in him, and if he find yo azz, he gon' murder you too" Ciera shook her head at how green Nita was.

"Yeah, don't be dumb" Tiera added.

"Well since you hoes so sprung on killin' him, won't y'all do it?" she said believing that would make them back down and let it be, but she should've known better. "Bitch, say no mo" Ciera said, resolute.

"How much money he got?" Tiera went straight for the finances.

"Let's just say if we do it, we'll be straight" Nita said while nodding her head up and down. "So how y'all planning on doing it?" she added.

"Well, the nigga do got some size to him compared to us, so it's gon' be hard for me to stab his azz because he already gon' be heated when he see me after the shit I said about him, so that'll likely turn into a wrestling match over the knife, and I ain't tryna do that, so I say we shoot his azz" Ciera said liking that idea.

"We ain't got no fuckin' gun" Tiera exclaimed.

"Oh, it's guns in this house, so don't even worry about that, y'all just be ready when that time comes" Nita said while getting up from the couch and going to stand directly in front of the TV, then she turned around. "We gotta make sure that we do this right, and make it look like a robbery because that police called me by my first name, so I know they gonna try to find me and question me" she continued.

"Don't even worry about it, I'll have the perfect plan by the time he gets home" Ciera said while thinking.

"Yeah, we got this, we gon' take care of this nigga, and then hop on the freeway back to the Chi" Tiera said loving that they were about to do some treacherous shit.

"What if JC still wit him?" Nita asked.

"Then we kill his azz too, fuck it. He had some good dick, but he may not ride with us against his guy, so he may have to go too" Ciera kept it real.

"It's a go then, let's go upstairs so that I can get the gun for y'all" Nita said and walked off as they followed close behind.

******

Richie Rich and JC drove to Richie's house on 42nd & Green Tree where Richie put the Cutlass in that garage, got the money that he had stashed over there, and hopped in his Benz. Then they drove to Richie's stash house on 39th & Lloyd, pulled up in the alley behind the house, where Richie got the rest of the cash he had stashed over there, then they grabbed the kilos and put them in the Benz's stash spot, and now they were heading back to Richie's house in Wauwatosa. As they pulled up to the lights on Sherman Boulevard & Lisbon, Richie turned the music up, and "Duck Tape" by Wooh Da Kid came on.

"This that shit!" Richie said as he bobbed his head before starting to rap word for word:

Turn it up a notch

Speed it up a tab, keep my mouth duck taped

I will never rat

Never squeal

No, I will never tell

I'd rather see a box

Or spend my life in jail...

The whole time Richie was rapping and looking out of his driver side window, JC was staring at the back of his head pissed the fuck off. *How the fuck could this nigga rap some real shit like this, and the police dropping this nigga off at the crib? He the fuckin' police...* JC thought to himself as Richie drove off. He was trying to keep his emotions under control, so that he could get his work and get outta town before Richie turned Fed against him.... but first, he needed to calm his nerves. Pulling out a pack of cigarettes, he hit it on the palm of his hand which turned Richie's attention towards him, then he opened the pack and pulled one out while cracking his window.

"My nigga, you not finna smoke that stankin' azz shit up in here" Richie said flat out.

"So, what the fuck I'm 'posed to do?" JC said irritated because he already felt like Richie was up to something behind his back, so his emotions were getting the best of him. "Smoke this, nigga!" he said.

Richie caught the aggression in JC's tone, but he knew all of the events that were going on had JC frustrated and so was he, so Richie let that go as he reached under the base of the steering wheel and pulled out a plastic bag with already rolled blunts in it. Pulling one out, he passed it to JC, but by then JC had already gotten himself worked up and had to get it off his chest.

"Say, nigga" JC said reaching to turn the radio down. "Imma say this, you on the phone whispering to yo bitch in code talkin' bout have this and that ready. I hope you ain't on no police azz shit, cause I'm telling you..." he added.

Richie Rich mugged JC while tryna keep his eyes on the road. He couldn't believe that he just came at him like that, and the reaction just flowed out the only way Richie knew how to handle things. "I'm saying, you telling me what, pussy azz nigga" Richie spat venom.

"Who the fuck you talking to, nigga!" JC yelled.

"It's only one of us in here wit a pussy and it smell like you bleeding" Richie said as JC tried to swing on him, but Richie moved out of the way just in time, then he sped up and pulled into an alley. "Get yo bitch azz out the car" he continued.

"You ain't saying shit I ain't wit" JC said snatching the handle to open the door, getting out, he slammed the door as he and Richie walked around to the front of the car. Soon as he was in striking distance, JC rushed Richie and connected with a right cross that sent Richie stumbling backwards.

"Yeah, bring yo bitch azz on" JC said while hopping side to side on his toes in his boxer's stance. Then he rushed Richie again throwing several punches, some of which caught Richie on the chin, side of the head, and in the shoulder as Richie stepped back to find JC's punching sequence, so that he could use it against him. JC stepped forward and tried to hit Richie with a left jab and a right cross, but Richie side stepped the jab and caught the cross with his for left forearm, then he punched JC in the stomach before scooping him up and dropping him. Then Richie jumped on JC and hit him hard as hell square in the nose as blood instantly shot out. As Richie was about to hit him again, JC caught him off-guard by putting his legs up and bringing them down quickly using his momentum to buck like a bull and get Richie off of him.

After Richie fell to the side of him, JC rolled over and got to his feet quickly, then he kicked Richie who was still down, and followed those kicks up with massive blows to Richie's upper body and head. The blows were so forceful, that it caused Richie's head to bounce off the concrete several times as he started to bleed and feel like JC was gonna try to kill him. "I told yo bitch azz I wasn't playing" JC said and kicked him several times, then Richie mustered enough strength and pulled the pistol from his waistband and pointed it at JC.

"Get yo bitch azz back" he said.

"What the fuck you gon' do wit that?" JC asked as he kept coming closer, so Richie showed him just what he was gonna do. JC grabbed his chest as he gasps for air when the slugs impacted with his chest and blood gushed out. Getting a short breath of wind, JC charged again and Richie fired again. T sent JC crashing to the ground. Richie hopped up and walked over to his lifeless body.

"Take this too, bitch azz nigga" Richie said then he kicked him. Rushing back to the car, Richie hopped in, and quickly smashed off without having his tires squeal. Then he reached for his cellphone in the cupholder.

******

Walsh was relieved that Gomez was no longer his shadow, and although he was supposed to have a partner, he preferred to work alone, he didn't need anyone seconding his decisions or throwing a monkey wrench in his plans. He was sitting at his desk going over some paperwork from the murder outside of PT's strip club that Richie Rich used to frequent, when he came across a statement from Tim, the owner of that club, the night one of the strippers was killed. "What do we have here?" he said out loud to himself as he began to read.

A young cat name Rich, hustler type of dude, real flashy, I catch him beating my dancer Peaches up. I tell him that ain't gon' fly in my establishment and went to get security to remove him from the club. Then I hear him tell Peaches he gon' fuck Jazzie up, my other dancer, if he find out that she had anything to do with Jazzie's boyfriend taking taking his money. I guess they 'posed to robbed him or something, I gave the detective my video surveillance footage...

Putting the paper down, Walsh couldn't help but smile as he made his way to the video room and told the video guy what he was looking for. As he waited the couple of minutes for him to put it on, he knew this was the evidence that he needed to take Richie Rich's azz down. As the video came on, one woman come out of the club followed by another woman, both of whom Walsh knew because he knows this case. The two seemed to have been engaged in an argument, when they begin to tussle, and one pulled out a knife and stabbed the other. Then she was standing around obviously grief stricken when a figure in dark clothing appears outta nowhere and Walsh knows it's Richie Rich as he calls the woman over and they get in the car and leave.

"You son of a bitch" he said out loud as everything had just become crystal clear. The woman who got in the car with him was the same woman they found at Lincoln Park dead from a single gunshot wound to the head, this is the same night Richie Rich's best friend got shot and burned in Washington Park. Ballistics matched and concluded they were killed from the exact same weapon, and he was last seen with her. "I got your azz now" he added. "Thanks, that's all I needed" he continued as he patted the video guy on the shoulder. Going back to his office, he grabbed his FBI jacket, and went to round up the troops to go bring Richie Rich in for good this time.

******

"Y'all stand right here with the gun, Imma try to get the gun he got on him away from him too" Nita said showing Tiera and Ciera where they needed to stand as her cellphone rang. "Shhh, this Richie... Hello" she said.

Aye, we gotta get going double time, so make sure you got everything ready, Imma run in and change my clothes, then we outta here, he said and she could tell that something was wrong with him.

"What's wrong?" she asked, flustered.

Nothin', now listen closely, he said then told her where to find some money he had hidden in the wall in the living room. *You got that?* he added.

"Yeah" she replied.

Aight, I'll be there in a minute, he said then hung the phone up.

Nita threw her phone on the bed as she told the twins that he was on his way. She thought about taking her clothes, but she knew that would look too suspicious, so she told the twins to pack some of her things in the suitcase that she pulled out of the closet, so it could look like she was just going outta town for a couple of days. After assigning them that task, she went downstairs to look for the money that Richie said he had stashed in the wall. Moving the small table out of the way, she saw a small compartment that was just below the stairwell. Bending down, she pulled the little piece of string that was peeking out causing the 12x12 square wooden door to fall down. Her eyes were wide as hell when she saw the bundles upon bundles of money neatly stacked one on top of the other.

"Oh... my... gawd" she said thinking just how much money he had. Standing up, she ran into the kitchen and grabbed a garbage bag from the box and bolted back into the living room, getting on her knees, she started stuffing the money in the bag. She could hear one of the twins calling her, but she was focused on securing the money. She didn't know how much it was, but when she tried to lift it...it was a real struggle as she had to slide it to the closet by the front door and put it in there along with the other bag of money. Wiping away the sweat from her forehead, she ran back upstairs two steps at a time, and went back into her bedroom where the twins were. "What was y'all calling me for?" Nita asked.

"Bitch, why you so outta breath?" Tiera asked.

"I had to run up all them damn stairs" she shot back. "What's up?"

"You want us to leave this suitcase here or take it downstairs?" Tiera asked.

Nita stood there momentarily while biting her fingernail. "Leave it in here, so I know that he has to come in here because the plan is to get him in this room" she told them.

"That makes sense" Ciera spoke, then the room fell silent as they were waiting for the inevitable. The more that they waited on Richie Rich to arrive, Nita began to feel uneasy about the whole ordeal as she sat on the bed looking at her friends. She loved Richie and didn't wanna kill him, but how could she go against her lifelong friends? She couldn't, and it was eating her up on the inside. Tiera sat there in complete silence while Ciera didn't say anything either, she had this look on her face that said it all. She had a confident and eager demeanor as she clutched the pistol in the palm of her hand. Then the phone rung and snapped all women in the room back to reality.

"This him!" Nita said as she walked over to the bathroom door that was connected to their master bedroom. Taking a deep breath, she cleared her throat, and got her composure together before answering the phone. "What's up, bae?"

I'm finna pull up in like two minutes, you got everything together? he asked.

"Damn near...I jus—"she said.

I told you to have that shit ready! You know what, I'll do it my muthafuckin' self when I get there, he yelled then hung the phone up on her before she could even utter another word.

Richie Rich knew he had to get the fuck outta Milwaukee, he had his mindset on going south, maybe to South Beach as he began mapping things out in his head from his specific choice of travel, to where they'd sleep, to the type of home he wanted to buy, and how he would continue to stay under the radar. But, he had to get all of his shit together. He didn't have time to collect his money from the lil niggas he had pushing that work for him, but he wasn't tripping on that, from his mental calculations, he had either just above half a million or close to it. So, he was good with that, he couldn't let Walsh make good on his promise to lock him up for good. "Definitely not getting me like that" he said out loud to himself as he pulled up in front of his house and backed into the driveway, hopped out, and ran in the house.

Walking through the door, he looked by the stairwell and saw the wooden structure down, so he knew Nita already got the money out as he started to call her. "Nita!" as he ran up the stairs.

******

"When we get there, I want the house secured and the perimeter locked down. This fucker is not getting away this time" Walsh said to one of the agents in the car with him.

"Sir, how many are we apprehending?" one of his agents asked.

"We'll round the entire house up, but mainly Richard Williams and James Cooper, those are the targets.

"Yes, sir" another agent replied.

******

When Richie Rich got upstairs, Nita was coming out of the bathroom buttoning up her shirt. "What you doin'?"he asked with a weird look on his face. She didn't answer him as she glanced down at his clothes noticing they were in disarray and that he had blood on his shirt.

"What happened to you?" she asked.

"Don't worry 'bout that, get yo shit so we can go" he ordered her.

Nita knew she had to find a way to get that gun from him, hit wasn't going as planned so far, and she knew if he walked in that bathroom, he'd see Tiera and Ciera flush against the wall barely out of sight, so she went to the closet and grabbed him a shirt and pair of jeans to put on.

"Richie, change outta that hot azz shit you got on, and put this on" she said and dropped the clothes on the bed. He thought about it and knew that she was right as she allowed her to help him remove his shirt. Then he pulled the pistol from his waistband and tossed it on the bed before he started unbuckling his belt and unbuttoning his pants. Sitting on the

215

bed, he leaned over and united his shoes. As he did that, Nita knew this was her only chance as she snatched the pistol from the bed and ran towards the bathroom causing Richie to look and wonder what all of her sudden movements were about.

"What the fuck is you doing?" he said as he saw her enter the bathroom and Ciera stepped out with the Glock aimed at his head with Tiera right behind her.

"I'm sorry, Richie, I had to choose my girls" Nita pleaded.

"Bitch, shut that shit up, yo punk azz prolly was planning this shit the whole time. But that's my fault for tryna wife yo rat thot azz, this how you repay me, bitch?" he said getting to his feet.

"Shut all that shit up, you thought you was finna just snitch and get my girl jammed up in that shit you got goin' on…not today" Ciera said.

"What the fuck you bitches keep talking about this snitch shit for? You hoes better quit playing wit me "Richie Rich exclaimed while walking around the bed.

"Don't move again, nigga" Ciera said as Tiera stepped off to the side and Nita gradually made her way by the door.

"Or what?" he said tryna determine how he was gonna get over to her and grab that gun without getting shot. He paused for a second, then without warning, he rushed Ciera throwing two hay makers to her face but not before she got off two shots. The bullets hit him in the torso and the upper left side of his chest causing him to stagger forward. He still managed to grab the gun as they wrestled over it while they fell to the floor. Even with being shot, he was still stronger than her, rolling over, he positioned himself on her chest as he looked into her eyes.

"You. Shot me, you punk azz bitch" he winced in pain.

"Get the fuck off my sister!" Tiera yelled and lunged towards him. Richie raised the gun and fired a single round into her face.

"NOOO!" Nita screamed as she watched her friend be thrown back into the wall from the force of the face shot and slid down it into her death. Nita's survival instincts took over at that point as she bolted down the stairs, and straight to the closet where she stashed the money at. Grabbing the lighter one of the two, she threw it over her shoulder, went outside, and seen the Benz blocking the garage where her truck was.

"Shit!" she said as she opened the Benz's door, looking in the ignition, as luck would have it, the keys were still in the ignition. Hitting the locks, she opened the back door, and put the bag in the backseat. The Benz was in her name anyway, so she was going to take that. Running back in the house, she listened, and didn't hear anything, at that point she didn't give a fuck as she drug the other bag out to the car taking baby steps.

******

Ciera was still conscious, but barely holding on because Richie had his forearm pressed against her neck. He was already on top of her, so it made it that much harder for her to breathe. Richie dug deep to stay alive even though he could feel himself slipping in and out of consciousness. Leaning over just inches from Ciera's face, he looked into her crying eyes.

"I'm dying" he said over coughs and hard choking noises trying to keep the blood from coming up." But ...you shot me, so...you dying... too" he growled out as he raised the gun and replaced his forearm with the gun and pressed it so hard that it caused her head to tilt back, then he pulled the trigger devilishly. The top of her head flew across the room as he collapsed on top of her exhaling his last and final breath.

******

Nita had just gotten the bag into the backseat, closed the door, and flinched when she heard the shot. Tears streamed down her face as she shook her head regretting even getting involved in the situation all together, she hoped that Ciera would come running out, but she knew that would never happen. Getting in the driver's seat, she started the car, and looked at the house one last time as the tears continued to fall. "I'm so so... sorry, Ciera... Tiera... and Richie, it's all my fault" she said before she wiped her eyes, sniffled and dropped the gearshift into drive and pulled off disappearing into the night.

******

About five minutes later, Walsh pulled up with the rest of the taskforce. They all hopped out, then after getting a last-minute briefing on how they were to handle this situation, they split up into two teams. One team would approach from the front and the other from the back, then they rushed in the house with their weapons drawn. "Clear" one of the agents yelled after they secured the bottom of the house, they made their way upstairs. When they made it to the top of the stairs, the lead man gave the signal to check the rooms on both sides of them while he proceeded down the hallway with Walsh right behind him. Getting to the last door, they peaked in as the other agents came and joined, then they entered the room and secured it.

"Clear" one of the agents yelled as Walsh put his gun away. He saw three DOA, one with her face missing, and two laid directly in the middle of the floor, one on top of the other. The only thing that was going through Walsh's head was how Richie Rich had managed to get away again. "Son of a bitch" he said as he knelt down to push the gun away from the person's hand that was on the floor. Upon a closer look, he tilted his head sideways trying to see if he could identify any of the people by face. He made a hypothesis that the ladies had to be that set of twin girls that Richie Rich's girlfriend ran around with, or that was Richie's girlfriend, her face was missing, so the identity would have to be determined at a later time.

Walsh looked up at one of the other agents and shook his head, believing that Richie Rich had gotten away with not only another homicide, but a triple homicide at that, he instantly wanted to blame Gomez. Turning back around, he rolled the body over that was on top of the woman who laid on the floor. He couldn't believe it when the head flipped around. Putting his hand atop his head, he let out a long sigh of disappointment as he looked down at Richie Rich's lifeless body. "Well, I'll be damned" Walsh said while shaking his head. "Call it in" he continued talking to one of his field agents.

To be continued.....

Live by It, Die by It (By: Ice Money)

Mercenary (By: Ice Money)

The Ruler of the Red Ruler (By: Kutta)

The Trenches: Murder, Money, Betrayal
(By: Kutta)

Block Boyz (By: Juvi)

Team Savage (By: Ace Boogie)

Team Savage 2 (By: Ace Boogie)

Team Savage III (By: Ace Boogie)

Love Have Mercy (By: Kordarow Moore)

Rich Pride (By M.L. Moore)

Available at Bagzofmoneycontent.com and most major bookstores.